ADAM GNADE

The Internet Newspaper

-Andrew Mears, of the band Youthmovies, author of *Kettledrum*

"The thing about Adam's work is that he's writing for you—writing for himself and because he must, like all good writers do—but for you and for us, with care and craft and love, he's documenting the mystery and the beauty of this glorious and shit world in a sweet punk rock symphony that absolutely makes it easier to keep living here."

-Nicole Morning, author of *Self-Titled*

"Adam Gnade is incredible at capturing the festering sickness at America's core, and the vulnerable want for something better."

-Jon Nix, filmmaker, TurnStyle Films, photographer, *Shy No More*

"To read Gnade is to get good and clobbered during the struggle between the world and the individual, history and the present moment, transcendence and total despair—but you come up grinning, tonguing the new holes in your messed up grill."

-Nathaniel Kennon Perkins, author of *Wallop*

"The power in Adam Gnade's work comes after the winds shift as the earth burns, despair looms, execs conspire and the gods take their bloody cut, the night army of cats snatch up all our tongues. There will be these words plain as death and the day after still summoning in us our fight."

-Rich Baiocco, author of *Torch Ballads*

"I told Adam Gnade that everyone hates me. He said I was being ridiculous—everyone hasn't met me yet."

-the ghost of Rodney Dangerfield, author of *It's Not Easy Bein' Me*

"To me, Adam Gnade is the warmhearted-anarcho-farmer-punk embodiment of the old mantra, 'do no harm/take no shit,' and that always seems to be an important reminder I take from his writing."

-Becky DiGiglio, photographer, *Born Upside Down*

"Adam's work is a superlative portrait of a world in which I want to live, to breathe, to eat of, and to swim in: complicated and broken but made whole by a raconteur's charming song of California sun, moshpit sweat, the foods of gods, and midwestern solace."

-andrw fx, author of *every thing* and *the absurd one*

"The motion picture *Hard Target* (1993, dir. John Woo) is based on Adam Gnade's life, with Gnade's knee-slapping yarns and jaw-dropping physical prowess inspiring the characters of both 'Chance Boudreaux' (Jean-Claude Van Damme) and 'Uncle Clarence Douvee' (Wilford Brimley). The next time you come across a rattlesnake in the Louisiana bayou, and the next time that rattlesnake latches onto your face, its needle-sharp fangs pumping venom into your veins as its tail crushes your windpipe, remember this: Adam Gnade knew you were coming. He put that rattlesnake there. And you deserve whatever you have coming to you."

-Henrik Eriksen, BrimleyWatch.biz

"Adam writes like a close friend opening up to you eight hours into a twelve hour drive down the coast, with a lighthearted candidness that makes you turn down the radio and say, 'Well, shit, now I'm invested.'"
-Erik Tinsley, author of *A Little Bit*

"Adam Gnade's writing is expansive and unrelenting; like your favorite anthemic songs, it'll make you want to raise your first in the air and fight back against the bullshit."

-Jessie Lynn McMains, Bone & Ink Press, author of *Wisconsin Death Trip*

THE INTERNET NEWSPAPER

[A NOVEL]

ADAM GNADE

THREE ONE G / BREAD & ROSES PRESS

Three One G/Bread & Roses Press
ISBN: 978-1-939899-45-3
First paperback edition, February 14th, 2023

Edited by Jessie Duke
Research assistance from Elizabeth Thompson
Art and layout by Bran Black Moon
Printing by KC Book Manufacturing

Printed in the United States of America
1 3 5 7 9 10 8 6 4 2

Down we go
Cradle and all
-X

The sunrise, the sunsets
You're hopeful, then you regret
The circle never breaks
-Bright Eyes

It's no surprise
Just how low
Some will go
-The Locust

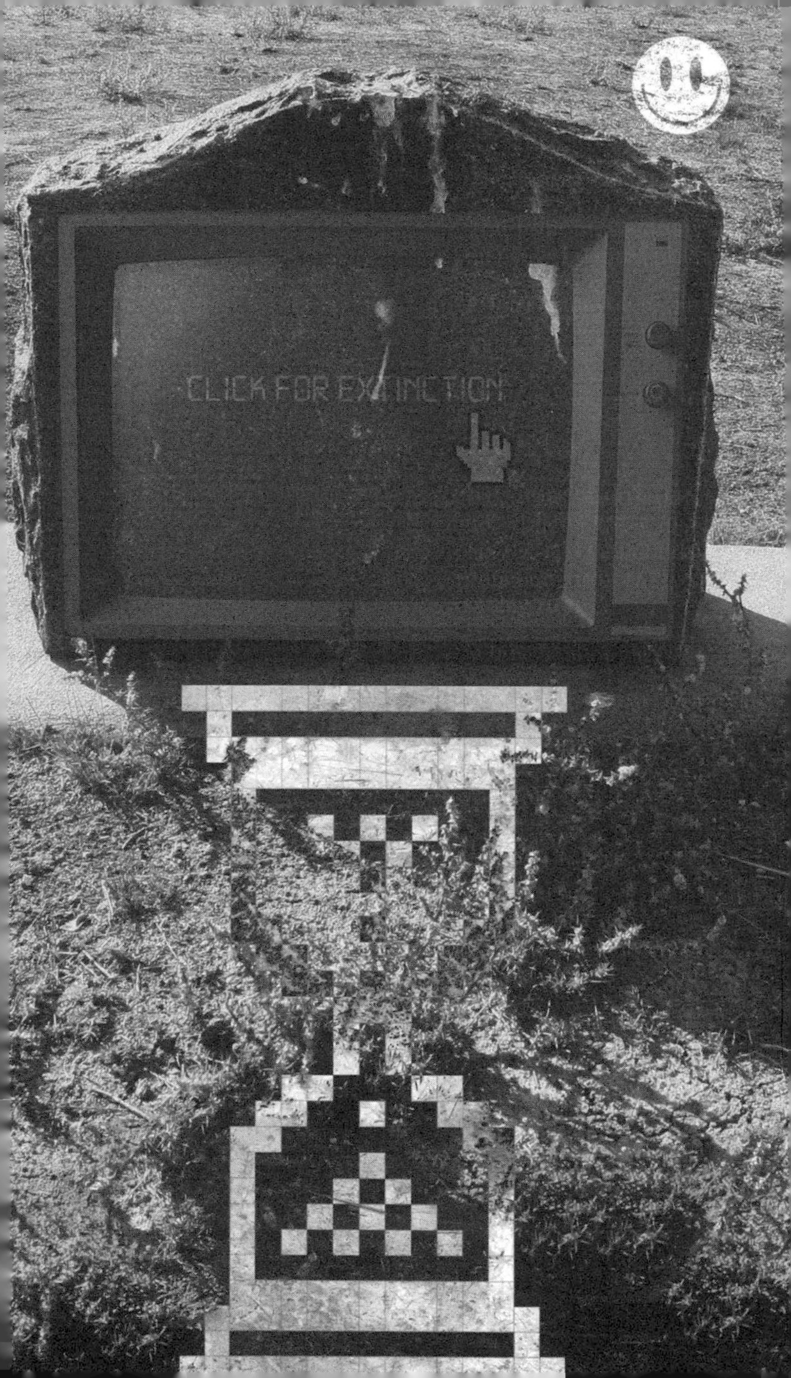
CLICK FOR EXTINCTION

Monday, October 2nd, 2000

You can see the palm trees from the third-floor windows of the internet newspaper. It's a bright, hot, gray morning in October—windy, the breeze lashing at the palms, bending their tall, thin trunks.

From where I sit in my dark blue folding chair in the conference room you don't hear the wind or the shaggy heads of the palms rustling or their trunks creaking. You don't feel the wind either. You feel the air-conditioning and you hear Brendan who's in charge of today's sales meeting standing in front of the white board talking to us about cats.

Brendan tells us how Jay wrote his column Friday and mentioned his cat and put a photo of it at the top of the piece above the headline and how the column had 51,563 hits over the weekend compared to last week's average of 32 hits a day.

"Nobody knows why but people want cats on the internet," says Brendan. "We want you to put *cats* in your stories. *If* you can. *Whenever* you can."

One of the news guys sitting in the row in front of me sticks his hand up like he's in a classroom.

"Chris," says Brendan, nodding patiently like a teacher, arms folded across his chest in a way that seems protective.

The news guy, Chris, gets to his feet and says, "Brendan, seriously, man. We're not a *pet magazine*."

"Chris. I know. But look—"

"We're a *newspaper*. We handle *news*. Not—not *animal stories*." Chris is one of the older news guys. He wears a suit every day. This one's light blue, long out of fashion like something you'd find in a thrift store and laugh about with your friends before putting it back. The jacket and pants are a couple sizes too big on his small frame and because of that he looks like a kid in a wedding suit. Chris says, "I didn't sign up for this," and Chris says, "Ugh, Jesus Christ, man," and Chris says, "You hear what you're *saying*, right?"

As Chris talks, Brendan does a very slow shrug that's so exaggerated it's like a vaudeville act which works because Brendan looks

1

like a ventriloquist's dummy—the empty blue eyes painted on the wood, the brittle-looking short curly brown hair, the oversized mouth that clops open and clops shut, and now Brendan's talking again and his squeaky voice hurts my stomach. "Look. *Chris*. Goal here's *traffic*. Traffic is money." He spells the word out for emphasis, and does it slow and lusty like, "Em oh en ee *why*." A disgusting smile spreads across Brendan's pink face. Brendan has small, rounded, spaced-apart peg teeth like a cartoon dinosaur and whenever you see them you feel like you're seeing something you're not meant to. He says, "More traffic means more ads which means us *charging* more for ads."

"Yeah. Sure. I get that but Brendan—"

"Chris, hear me out. The paper making more money means more money for us and I *know* you guys want raises, right? Am I right?" Brendan looks around the room, arms spread like Jesus welcoming the children. He waves his hands upward in a "Come on now" motion, soliciting confirmation and agreement from us in editorial who sit stone-faced, impassive. "I mean, right? *Guys. Raises.*" He stamps his foot in a way that's supposed to be inspirational. "We all wanna get that cash *money*. Goal's to double ad numbers by New Year's Day 2001. We've got two months. New Year's. January 1ˢᵗ. Wham. The big goal."

As he sits back down Chris the news guy throws his hands in the air like everything is futile, like life is shit.

The room is quiet now except for the sound of the A-C blowing through the vents.

Outside, the breeze bends the palm trees silently.

Someone in the back coughs, but it doesn't sound like a real one. It sounds like a cough to clear the tension, to fill up the space.

Brendan shuts his lifeless ventriloquist dummy eyes and brings his hands together under his chin then his eyes snap open. "Oh! You guys! The bell!" he shouts. "I almost forgot! We finally got the bell!" Brendan's arms shoot above his head, and he makes Olympic gold medal victory fists as the front two rows of salespeople clap and cheer.

A stocky, brown-haired one whose name I can never remember stands up and pumps his fist in the air in a circular motion and barks, "Woof! Woof! Woof!"

I call the woofing guy "Donut" because he always shouts, "*Who brought donuts?!*" in the morning when he walks in from reception. No one ever brings donuts. No one brings anything for anyone. That doesn't matter. Donut is forever hopeful about donuts and unabashedly loud with his hope and I hate him for it.

The only thing Donut loves as much as donuts is doing things in slow motion to make people laugh.

I imagine how good it would feel to stand up and scream.

No words. Just a scream.

Scream until everything goes white.

Like he's done at meetings more times than I can count, Donut slow motion jogs up to Brendan as if he's been running for hours and he's exhausted, at the same time reaching out for a slow motion high-five, saying, "Hiiiiigh-fiiiive" in a slow, deep voice.

Everyone in sales loves it.

They laugh.

A few people clap.

Someone sitting up front I've never met says the words "slow motion" in slow motion and that gets more laughs.

Brendan bends down behind the plastic folding table in front of the white board looking for something in a row of cardboard boxes while Donut turns and gives fast, violent high-fives to the front row of salespeople—fast to punctuate how slow he was moving before. The slow then fast thing is part of the game. With each fast smack of the hand he shouts, "Yeee-ah!" Six of them. Six "Yeee-ah!"'s and the sixth "Yeee-ah!" also gets a "Bro!" at the end like a thunderclap, like a warhammer hitting a shield in some rainy, blood-splattered, mythological tale.

After that Donut does a few bodybuilder poses for some reason with a grim, intense look on his face like he's straining hard to shit while everyone in sales cheers him on.

"Pumped!" says Donut clapping his hands once and hard.

Brendan stands back up and sets a large cardboard box that

looks heavy on the table. "Oh you guys. I am so happy to present—drum roll everybody—the bell! The bell! The bell!" he
shrieks proudly.

One of the salesgirls, an awful, sour-faced blonde called "Sind"
gets up and helps Brendan. They reach into the box, and each
taking a side, lift a brass bell the size of a soup pot out and set
it on the table.

"Thanks, Sind!" shouts Brendan. "Wham! The bell's here!"
Brendan's voice gets shrill when he's excited, and he's excited
most of the time. His voice is harsh, thin, and high. The weird
part is I've heard Brendan serious before and there's something
scary about his serious voice. It's deeper—his diction slow and
measured as he makes sure to carefully choose each word. He
doesn't say "Wham" when he's serious and he doesn't say "Oh
you guys!" It's unsettling that Brendan's excited voice is an affec-
tation. When you hear him serious you want to leave the room.
It's like seeing a snake on the trail ahead of you—all your instincts scream "TURN. BACK. NOW."

I can feel the tension build—the arts and entertainment staff,
our boss Ed, the news guys, the associate editors we rarely see,
their (our) tension hangs around us like a poisonous cloud.

"Swear to fuckin' *god* I'm gonna squat down and take a *piss* in
that bell," I hear Emily Benowitz whisper behind me.

I turn to look and Emily smiles at me and mouths, "Fuck the
bell" with a swaggering, happy-to-be-angry snarl. When Emily's
angry her red hair looks like fire and her green eyes shine like
something beautiful, vile, and deadly. I drag a finger across my
throat and make a dead face like "Oh just kill me now" and we
both laugh without making any noise. "Dude. *Fuck* the bell,"
she says louder this time, and I turn back just as Brendan hits
the side of the bell with a piece of metal that looks like a brass
crowbar.

I startle so badly I drop my empty coffee mug on the floor.

Before I can reach down for it my mind tells me to give up.

Give up.

It tells me to give up about the mug just like it told me to give up
about getting out of bed this morning and give up about being

alive, which it's told me more times than I can count lately.

Give up.

Give.

Up.

When I'm going through a bad spot like I am now, it's as if my mind and I are too different people. It hates me and I hate it. We're at war. At best we're like baby siblings arguing over who owns the red shoe or whose turn it is to use the special chair. Mostly the war rages on with spectacular violence. The war is like a volcano that will turn the world to ash. The world in question is me. The war and the volcano are me as well. The product of this equation is a dumb, self-defeating shitstorm.

"Okay! The bell plan!" Brendan says. "Sales knows this already, of course, but for editorial's sake the way it works's we get a new ad then we—bang! Ring the bell. For a normal sale we ring it with the rope thing like, y'know, ding-a ling-a ling." He laughs with a terrible rolling peel of *hee hee hee hee* noise that feels like rats scrabbling around in the pit of my stomach trying to chew their way out. "For a *big* sale we use the crowbar. Bang! That's how we know we're excelling and that the health of the site is—" he's at a loss for words. He looks down at his knobby pink hands then looks up at us and I know he doesn't want to say "healthy" because he's already said "health" but that's all he's got and he laughs a little and smiles his wide grin with his little round teeth and says, "—we'll know the site's healthy."

I like to imagine smashing Brendan's head.

Sometimes it's a melon and I have a sledgehammer and the seeds and pulp spray everywhere like how I expect the Big Bang looked.

Sometimes I push a giant stone off a cliff in the way they killed Piggy in *Lord of the Flies*.

Today I imagine crushing his head in my hands like a ball of tin-foil—crushing it down to the smallest possible size then dropping it in a toilet and flushing him into the sewers of San Diego.

After the sales meeting we go to Asia Feast Buffet in Fashion Valley for Ed's birthday lunch. Ed O'Connell is Brendan's uncle which is how Brendan got the job. Even though Brendan is Ed's nephew, they're nothing alike. Ed isn't popular at work, but he's a great guy—kind, valiant, though a little clueless. He's fatherly and patient and he loves the staff no matter how they feel about him.

Ed oversees the entire editorial operation. The paper's his baby. You'd never hear him say that. He's humble. Doesn't take the power too seriously. Ed's older, but he frets over his appearance, and because of that you can't tell his age. I'm 24. Ed's 60, but he's in better shape than any of us. He was a college football star and plays over-the-line on weekends and swims at the Plunge every day after work. He's bald except for the sides like Skinner from *X-Files,* and today he's wearing a yellow button-up shirt with a silver-blue tie, khaki slacks, and he's got the kind of red-brown tan you get when you grow up in San Diego and never use sunscreen.

He's a little vain, but it seems more a matter of pride than egotism, like he holds himself to high standards because why shouldn't you? I like Ed. We are complete opposites and maybe that's why I look up to him because I would rather be anything else than what I am. I know it's self-defeating, but I absolutely do *not* hold myself to high standards. I'm just trying to get through the day without throwing myself off the top of our building.

I joke about killing myself to my friends, but I joke about it to ease the reality of wanting to die. The desire to end it all is something I've had in me since middle school—this little voice pushing me on. *Do it. C'mon. You know you want to do it. Everything would be so much easier.*

It comes and goes. When it's gone I'm fine. On a good day I'm "genuinely, authentically happy" my friend Lil' Cassidy Nguyen calls me. When it's here it's something I can't ignore—a quiet, whispering voice that drowns out all else. It's been happening for so long I notice the patterns and that's something I force myself to remember. Four days, five days, get through that and you're in the clear. This week is the first I've had it in months. I woke up Monday morning with it. Woke up with that sick feeling in my stomach and the weight on my chest. When it's like this, when it gets bad, it makes the smallest problems so much harder, and a normal week becomes a shitty, ridiculous odyssey

6

where everything feels insurmountable. Usually I can take what comes. Not now.

The thought of being someone else is a thing I hide in. Often I daydream how different life would be, how easy and light to wake up without that weight, without the voice nagging me, forcing me to make plans, to consider my options for an easy, painless exit.

To be someone like Ed?

I can't even imagine how good that would feel.

Most of the news guys don't like Ed. They think he's pathetic because he used to work for the print version of the paper and has been pushed off to our corner of Mission Valley to rule over the third floor of the gray stone and black glass building just off Friars Road. They consider Ed a has-been, but they're all ex-Print too. Everyone here refers to the print version of the paper as "Print" like it's a person, an enemy sometimes, a parent to impress. Print as a thing to get to (or get back to). Print as a pitiless god or a cloud looming over us threatening rain.

Emily, who looks up to Ed in the same way I do, says the news guys are projecting because they're watching themselves slip into irrelevancy, that it's human to project the parts we don't like about ourselves onto other people, especially as we get older, and to take a smug sort of satisfaction in hating them for it. Being human is shit a lot of the time, but what else have we got? I'd like to start over. End this stupid life and find a new one. I think often of a line I love from James Baldwin, a refrain from his first novel, *Go Tell it on the Mountain.* Baldwin (writing in the character of Elizabeth Grimes) says, "I'm going away from here." When I think of that I remember a hymn I sang as a kid at North Park Seventh Day Adventist before my parents and I stopped attending, before I quit believing. We sang, "and now we shall go away from here." I'm going away from here. And now we shall go away from here. Away from here. On days like this it loops in my head like a chorus. Away from here. Away. From. Here.

I've been at the internet newspaper on a temping basis since earlier this year. Emily Benowitz and AJ Romano, who are a bit older than me, were hired to run the arts and entertainment section when the site launched two years ago, but all the news guys are decades-long veterans from Print. They were sent off with

Ed in '98 when the internet newspaper first opened, sent off for what Ed calls the paper's "little experiment in staying young."

If the news guys look down on Ed, they like Emily, AJ, and me even less. News considers our work less substantial than theirs. Of course the staff of the print version of the paper looks down on the staff of the online version. Editorial hates sales and the feeling from sales is entirely mutual though not as deep-seeded. The older people look down on the younger people and the younger people look down on the older people. Everyone hates everyone outside their age group or department. This is a universe of hate, an elaborate, many-tiered structure of people hating people.

Maybe because I'm new here (and haven't been beaten down as much as the rest of the staff) I don't hate anyone besides Brendan and Donut. I like Ed. I like most of the news guys even if they don't like me. I half-like the few salespeople I've met (and keep my distance from the rest). I like the associate editors who rarely leave their offices. Emily and AJ are great. They're both section editors, which is one step down from associate editor. I'm the only arts writer on staff. (My official title is "Content Producer," which sounds sterile and mechanical like a job title at a dog food factory.) The rest of the coverage is handed out to freelancers AJ and Emily hire. From what AJ says most of the freelancers hate the staffers because you get benefits on staff (unless you're temping like me. Most of the staff employees hate the freelancers because they think they're disorganized and lazy. The truth is we all wish we could work from home. Good things are rarely done in cubicles.

The only person universally loved is the front desk lady Monica who can do no wrong. Monica came here from Napoli a few years ago to marry a La Jolla stock trader who left her a month into their marriage and moved to Malibu with his bookkeeper. Half the guys and a few of the girls here at the internet newspaper are either in love or lust with Monica. She's very nice and taller than most of us and looks like a Hollywood actress from the 1940s. AJ dropped some nice gossip last week about how Monica dated someone from the Cure in the '80s but she won't talk about it and makes sure to change the subject when it's brought up. Regardless, it's pretty bad-ass, and those of us who love the Cure love Monica even more because of it. Monica is AJ's cousin, though AJ left Italy as a child and didn't know her when he lived there. Everyone here is here because of someone else. Brendan because of Ed. Me because I freelanced for the paper with Emily as my editor before being hired. I was very excited when offered the job. I'm not excited anymore.

And so the refrain plays.

Away from here.

Away from here.

At Asia Feast Buffet we take plates by the entrance and walk down the serving line. The room is cavernous like an airplane hangar and the line is U-shaped, bending along the edges of the room with men in white uniforms behind the tables refilling the tubs of food and cleaning up spills. You pay a flat fee at the front then follow the line which ends at the soda fountain and soft serve machine and a thing like a salad bar for the desserts.

In the middle of the U are tables. We've got a very long rectangular series of connected tables with 40 settings reserved for us. Most of the tables are smaller with settings for eight or four or six.

The place is completely full, and outside a line of people stand in the drizzling rain waiting to get in. "Pissy mist" is what AJ called it on the drive here. The windstorm from this morning brought mist and drizzle—gray, listless, gloomy drizzle once the wind died out.

I take a plate and shuffle along past the metal serving tubs labeled:

General Tso's chicken

Shrimp with vegetable

Kung pao shrimp

Egg foo young

Fried wontons

Chicken gyoza

Pork dumplings

Chicken wings

Pork eggrolls

Beef teriyaki

Crab legs

Sushi rolls

Tempura vegetables

Miso soup

Hot and sour soup

Wonton soup

Seafood delight soup

Egg drop soup

Vegetable fried rice (I put some of that on my plate)

Beef fried rice

Shrimp fried rice

Chicken fried rice

Pork fried rice

Vegetable lo mein (some of that too)

Beef lo mein

Shrimp lo mein

Pork lo mein

Almond chicken

Moo goo gai pan

Curry chicken

Szechuan beef

Mongolian beef

Moo shu pork

Coconut shrimp

Sweet and sour chicken

Mixed vegetables (some of that)

Sauteed fried broccoli (that too)

The chairs near Emily, AJ, and Ed are taken so I sit between two salesgirls I've never spoken with and pick at my lunch as the seats around us fill up.

There's a lot of turnaround in the sales department. Besides Brendan and Donut, who are sales executives, the staff of sales reps comes and goes, staying a few weeks, a month, then peacing out for better jobs or graduate school.

AJ and Emily have both dated a lot of salespeople. AJ says it's not shitting where you eat because no one in sales stays long enough to make it awkward. "Shitting where you eat" is one of AJ's favorite things to say. I don't like it because it makes it seem like dating is shitting. I brought that up to AJ once and he laughed and said, "Yeah, bro, but it's true. Dating is like taking a shit sometimes. Half the guys I date are either shit, toilets to shit into, or toilet paper to wipe your ass."

The salesgirls on either side of me are eating crab legs. It's all they've taken—a pile of orange and white exoskeleton limbs like something from a giant insect. They crack the shells in their hands and use the pointed ends of the claw to drag out the meat which they dip in clarified butter using a tiny fork like a Playmobil farm tool. While they break the shells open they talk about someone they know called Todd Platt.

"Ooh, yeah. *Man.* Todd fucking Platt. *He's* a baddie," says the salesgirl to my left.

"Todd Platt? People fucking *love* him. Nobody understands what a dick that guy is."

"Oh, *I* know. He came to Tasha's party and didn't say hi to *anyone.*"

"That's such a Todd Platt thing."

"*Total* Todd Platt thing. He walked in and was like, 'Duhhh, where's the good beer?' All he said. Didn't even say hi to Tasha. Didn't even say hi to me."

"You know who's cool? His sister."

"Carrie?"

"Noooo, Carrie Platt's a *bitch*. Kendra."

"Oh, yeah. Kendra. Totally. She's cool as hell."

"*Right?* Her tits are fake though."

"Oh yeah, for sure. Kendra's tits are *hella* fake."

"When I found out I's like, *Gross, yo*. I would never do that."

"Yeah, me neither. When *I* found out I was all, *Never, never, never*. I wouldn't do that to myself even if you paid me a million dollars."

"Yeah, never ever."

"She's cool though."

"Kendra? Super cool."

"She used to be a cunt a couple years ago. Remember that?"

"*Oh*. Right. When she was dating Alex from Coronado? Total cunt."

"I'm glad she's nice now."

"Meeee too."

"Wait. Didn't you *fuck* Alex from Coronado?"

"Me? Nooo. I gave him a blowjob after Ashley's party in his car."

"Ew, nooo. You didn't let him come in your mouth, right? He was *so gross*. Ick, Carly."

"*Yeah*, I let him. What else would I do? Anyway, I was faded off my *ass*. I barely remember."

"Oh my god I can't believe you let *Coronado Alex* come in your mouth. That makes me wanna *barf*. I could totally barf right now."

"I dunno. He was kinda hot in a creepy maybe-a-serial-killer way."

"No!"

"He was."

"No, no, no, no! Time out. Not at all. In *nooo* way whatsoever, Carly."

"I mean, *kinda* he was. Like a Ted Bundy way?"

"No! That is *so* wrong, Carly."

I lean close to my plate to stick a chopstick load of fried rice into my mouth, and as I do, I hear a crab leg snap open to the left of me and some of the liquid flicks against the side of my face.

It smells like salt and urine.

I sit up straight and wipe my face with my napkin and get up to leave.

As I'm pushing in my chair the salesgirl to my right holds her empty plate for me to take. She asks, "Can you grab me some of those pink Chinese cakes if you're getting up?"

I take the plate and walk to the exit just as Ed stands up to make a speech.

"Speech! Speech!" chants Donut in a fake deep voice like a football coach or a professional wrestler.

"Okay. Hi. Hi everyone. Thanks guys. I mean it. Thanks," says Ed, holding his hands out and waving them to quiet everyone down.

By the exit I set the salesgirl's plate in a gray bus tub. The glass doors slide open and I walk through them into the drizzle and gray.

Back from lunch we have an editorial meeting. It's just Ed and me at the big round table in the middle of our department. The news guys are off in their corner about to come over. You can hear them talking, but you can't make out the words.

"So, cats," says Ed smiling. "*Un*believable." The fluorescent lights shine off the lenses of his glasses and off his bald head. He says unbelievable again, but this time it's spaced apart like four words with emphasis in the middle rather than the beginning. "Un buh *leave* ible."

"Yeah. Cats, huh? Cats."

I have nothing to say. I'd rather write about anything than A&E. Cats, sure. Cats before music profiles and reviews. Cats before sports, which I can't stand anyway. Cats before nightclub parties, DJs, movies, bar crawls, art shows, restaurant openings, library events, book readings, operas, plays, and street fairs. Give me cats, Ed.

None of this I say out loud. I hardly ever say what I truly want to say. I'm aware of that, but—sometimes I just can't. I don't know why it won't come. It's like one of those nightmares where you're trying *so* hard to scream and you're absolutely voiceless and whatever's coming is coming for you with a *purpose* and nothing will stop its attack.

So, cats.

I'll write about cats.

Okay.

I surrender.

Send in the cats.

I realized my first week here I'm not a journalist. I want to write about my friends and myself. I want to make up stories about life as I know it, and I want to hide my own stories behind fiction. Ed knows this. He knows I'm going to quit. Knows I hate working for the internet newspaper. He's been trying his best for weeks to bring me back in, to keep me excited. Last week he gave me his personal copy of *I Cover the Waterfront,* Max Miller's book about working as a reporter in San Diego in the 1920s. Miller hated his job too and the book just strengthened my resolve to quit.

The main thing keeping me here besides rent and bills is I don't want to disappoint Ed. Sometimes with truly good, genuine people, the thought of hurting them (the thought of *anyone* hurting them) is absolutely overwhelming. You imagine them hurt and through some weird magic you feel that pain too.

Last week, over beers at the Alibi, AJ told me Brendan is seeing Ed's wife Stef, which apparently everyone but Ed knows.

"Brendan, his own goddamn nephew!" said AJ pounding his fist on the bar top like a Viking. "He should be killed for that, y'know? Just, like, *killed* in all the worst ways."

Stef's a lot younger than Ed. She's beautiful, and she's cool in a sort of reserved, dignified, royal way. Of course, the shock of finding out would destroy Ed.

AJ is right. Brendan should be killed in terrible ways. Sometimes I imagine swinging a sword on a battlefield and cutting Brendan's head from his shoulders—the slow-motion spray of blood misting the air, and as I fall to my knees in the wet, green grass, weary from the fight, the dark gray sky hanging above, Brendan's head hits the ground, rolls once, and his dead eyes stare up at me.

I feel like I should tell Ed about Brendan and Stef, but I can't bring myself to do it. Maybe it's not my place, or maybe it is. He needs to know, but does he need to know from me? I'm nothing, a temp, a kid.

As I stare at Ed across the table, while he shuffles through a stack of paper looking for his storyboard, I'm overcome with the kind of guilt that makes you dizzy, nauseous, and feverish. The kind of guilt that's as physical as it is emotional.

"So, James," Ed says, "before the guys get here, I wanted to see if—I think it's time for you to write a feature."

It takes me by surprise. "You want me to, like—*really*?" I feel myself blushing. It's embarrassing and I try to play it cool, be an adult.

"I think you're ready."

"I mean, yeah. Cool. *Sure*. Like on what?"

"That's what I want you to decide."

"You want me to drum up some, like—um, a list of ideas and you can—I dunno, pick one that I should write?"

"I don't want you to pitch me anything. This should be all you."

"All me, how?"

"You're younger than the rest of us."

"I guess but—"

"No, your world's different. The stuff you're into's different and—I don't know, man, I think bringing some of that into the paper would be good for us. Print—they want us to appeal to a younger audience. That's you. That's—y'know, it's where you're coming from."

"Whoa. Yeah, I guess."

"So, write it. Whatever it is. Let's say 1,000 words?"

"Okay."

"And turn it in Thursday.

"Thursday."

"—and if it's good enough Print will pick it up too. Then— *argh*, shit, man, maybe we can get you off temping and have you here permanently like everybody else. I'm trying. You know that, right?"

I nod. "Yeah. I do. Thank you."

"But we all know how it is over at Print. They don't do us any favors. They're just waiting for the fad to pass. A good feature would help."

"Okay, I can do that. For sure." I'm excited and it surprises me how excited I am, but I play it off. I don't want Ed to think I'm a baby.

I am, though.

A baby, I mean.

I've only had an email address since last year and my first day on the job I had to call my friend Joey Carr from a payphone outside and ask him what Ed meant by "Just copy and paste it."

I'm a dumb fucking baby who is still temping even though I work full time. A baby who gets through the day by faking it and calling friends about the technical stuff.

One of my biggest problems here at work is I don't care about the internet. AJ and Emily and even Ed are very much "internet people." They've been using it for years and they see it as "humanity's next big step" (AJ's words) and "really fucking exciting, James. I can't believe you don't *see* that" (Emily's). They invest themselves wholeheartedly in learning what's new to learn. They want to be up with all its latest advancements, to "know the game in order to win it" (AJ again).

What I want from life is something more earthbound. I want to drive around aimless with my friends or sit on porches or rooftops alone reading magazines. I want to go see weird bands play shows and I want to drink on curbs and write letters. I want summer heat and I want backyard swimming pools and I want ice-cold 40s and leisure time.

The life I lead outside of work is a much slower, simpler one— time spent alone or socializing in equal measure, endless attempts at writing fiction (on paper) between trips to 7-Eleven for beer and nachos, hours spent walking around the city looking at things and writing things down and taking my time.

Of course, I have to work because almost everyone has to work but this job? It's like a medicine I need to take each day to stay alive, a medicine that tastes like hell, but the end result of the untreated sickness would be eviction and going deeper into debt. Or maybe it's not a medicine. Maybe this job and most work we do is like an antidote to a poison that exists in almost all of us. For whatever reason or reasons we have been poisoned and in order to stay one step ahead of the toxic effects we must take the antidote.

I like writing lists but there's a difference between making lists and "scheduling." Work is a vast system of scheduling. It's also awful lighting like the glare shining off poor Ed's hairless scalp as he sits across from me saying words I hate like "synergy" and horrid, nightmare shit like "As far as your feature goes the only thing I would add—and this is such a small thing but something Print beats into us—is we need to focus on aligned messaging in order to make our content more cohesive before we start thinking outside the box." Work is everything plugged in and running at all times and the idea of that is exhausting. It's oppressive, inhuman, and sad.

When I leave work each day the life I live is not plugged into any wall. I know my free-time life is the better life and I know this in the most fundamental way. It's like knowing food keeps you alive, like knowing you have one left hand and one right, and that the way you taste things is with your tongue. It's the kind of thing you know without *having* to know or think much about and those are the truest things.

Emily sits down in the chair to the left of me smelling like strawberry lip-gloss and AJ sits to my right reeking of cigarettes and bad alcohol like an old man. Then the news guys file in wearing their shlumpy older guy suits that drag and hang at the cuffs. The news guys take the remaining seats, setting coffee mugs, notebooks, and manilla folders in front of them.

"Bill, you're not *drinking* that horse piss, are you?" says one of the news guys jutting his chin at the news guy to his left's coffee.

"Bill, you know I'll eat or drink anything that's free."

"You're sick, Bill. Go to a doctor."

The news guys call each other "Bill." I don't know why, but they use Bill so often I've only learned two of their names. There's Chris Yates, Jay Cerone (who put the cat in his column), and Bill Rosen (who might be called "Jeff" or maybe "John") along with Bill Ferguson, Bill Anaya, and Bill Besson. Chris, Jay, maybe a Jeff/John, and a bunch of Bills. Chris and Jay are of course Bills too, but I know their names because I've read their stories for years in the print version of the paper.

I would love to be a Bill, but it's not going to happen. Writing news, and I mean writing it well, is something that exists in the space between natural talent and years of hard work. The news guys' Bill club is a club for a reason. They've earned their place. That's a door shut to me—shut and locked. Good, clean news reporting (that rare combination of objective yet engaging) is a beautiful, important, noble thing. It's painful to admit you don't have what it takes, but I most definitely do not have the tools to be a journalist. (I'm less Woodward and Bernstein than I am flotsam and jetsam.)

Reading the daily paper was one of my favorite things as a kid. In the depths of middle school, in the ugly pit of high school, it was a friend. The big, thick, heavy, fragrant fold of pages, the newsprint smudging the tips of your fingers, the outer layers often damp from the morning dew, but what a world laid out before you—the tragedy and aspirations of humanity, our wars, our politics, cultural achievements, progress, the triumph of justice fulfilled, trials and crimes, our small victories, the bluster of the opinion pages, stocks rising and falling, empires in flux, deaths reported and mourned, and every day more of it than you could read—ongoing investigations like great detective stories, in-depth reporting, writing as clean and clear as a church bell ringing. The daily newspaper—the story of us, of our times, and each day presented anew, written and printed without cease or abeyance, a great novel of who we are, what we were, and where we are going (and why we are going there). The internet newspaper is less a ghost or shadow of that than a decaying 10th generation clone—fleshy, translucent, diminished to the point of malnourishment and disfunction. There is no glory, truth, or nobility here like there is at Print. This new kingdom is a rule on the wane.

Before I leave for the day I take my canvas KPBS tote bag into the supply room and steal office supplies—a box of red Sharpies, a brand-new pair of scissors still twist-tied to its backing card, three highlighters in colors I like (a soft neon blue, pale lilac, and a dusky magenta). After that I grab a box of staples that's so small it's cute, a staple remover shaped like a fanged set of jaws, and the best find of all: an old but perfectly good stapler with the original name of the newspaper before it merged with a rival paper and got the name it has today. The stapler was once white, but now it's that faded cream-gray that happens to old computer monitors and keyboards.

Walking back down the hall to my desk (because I forgot my car keys) I stop by Ed's office to wave goodbye, which he returns followed by a thumbs up as he talks on the phone, then I leave through reception, waving to Monica the beloved receptionist as I head out.

"Goodbye for today, James. I see you have *great* night," says Monica in the Naples accent and bad English that drives everyone wild. "I see you have great night" is a trademark Monica saying, as is her teasing you with "What are you doing? Making bread?" which means "What's taking you so long?"

The elevator is full of salesgirls talking about margaritas.

"It is sooo time for margos. Margos in the *house*. Margos gon fuck you up up *up*," says one of them, doing a little dance where she squats down with each repetition of "up" and waves her hands in front of her like she's polishing a window.

"Get faded off your aaaaaaass," sings another, dancing in place, pretending to smack the window polishing dancer on the ass. "BRANG THAT FAT ASS HERE BITCH!" she shouts straight up at the ceiling of the elevator, her face strained into a horrible contortion like she's on the electric chair, and they all laugh.

The elevator door slides open and I don't wait for them to get off like you're supposed to.

I charge forward and walk so fast to my car I'm almost jogging then 15 minutes later I'm drinking at the Livewire with Lil' Cassidy Nguyen.

Lil' Cass and I sit on bar-stools in the back by the pool tables drinking Tecate cans with a slice of lime. The beer is cold and foamy and the lime sour and it's the first time all day I've felt human.

Cass keeps excusing herself to do coke in the restroom and each time she comes back she's more excited about our plans for the night.

My plans were as follows:

-go home

-put on my trusty old Sugar Plant *After After Hours* CD and drink chianti from a basketball-size jug I bought half off at Hillcrest Ralph's yesterday

-after the wine begins to blur the edges I'll make a quesadilla with nine pounds of cheese and fry it in butter

-and sleep. No, more like SLEEP. Heavy. Much-earned. All-caps SLEEP.

Cassidy's housesitting this week at some fancy place in Del Mar and she wants me to come up there with her and hang out. The selling point is the pool, she says, telling me that it is literally impossible to say no to a pool like they have and that "Those muhfuckers got some *Gatsby* shit up in that bitch." I tell her my day was *so* long and she says, "Bitch, don't even *front*, my day was too." She goes on to tell me that "One of the dishwaters, this big ol' blonde hesher Hulk Hogan muhfucker Ben Purlo, came in fucked-up on speed and got in a fight with the Sysco delivery driver and pushed him down the loading dock stairs then—then fuckin' Purlo beat the hell out of him with a broomstick he broke in half over his knee like a fucking *maniac* and we had to call security but security never showed because they're lazy and stupid so we called the cops and the cops were all pissed off at us when they got there because fuckin' Purlo locked himself in the walk-in freezer and it just turned into a big ol' stupid circus."

Cassidy works as a server in the dining room of a retirement center up on Mount Soledad, which is how we met before I quit to work at the internet newspaper.

I tell her, "Cass, I'm *human* and humans need sleep." When I realize I'm complaining I try to turn it into a joke, saying, "You never sleep and that's fine with you because you're a vampire."

"Yez I em," she says in a vampire voice. "I em bampire." She flips the collar of her leather jacket up and pulls one side in front of her face and stares at me from behind it, dramatically, eyes wide and blazing.

"I can't keep up with your coke vampire lifestyle. It's exhausting."

"James, your *weakness* is exhausting. I have come here to do cocaine and kick ass and I'm *all* out of cocaine." Cass gives me a scary, bug-eyed look and punches her right fist into her left hand which makes me laugh.

"You're *never* out of cocaine and that's—see, there's your problem right there. They can't slow you down. You're the Unsinkable Lil' Cassidy Nguyen."

"Daaamn right, bee-otch."

"I'm mortal, Cass. I sink like a motherfucker. I'm sinking now. See—the water's—the water's right here—" I hold my hand right below my neck then raise it to my chin then to my nose and make gurgling noises. "Those are supposed to be gurgling noises like I'm sinking. See it's funny because I'm not actually underwater. I'm in a bar. The joke is funny because bars aren't underwater."

Cass ignores my explain-a-joke-to-death bit and takes a sip of her beer then snaps the tab off and flicks it at the wall. Whether it hits or not I can't tell. It's as if it absorbs into the darkness of the room and slips out of reality. "Ooh, I've got a bombshell for *you*, James."

"Oh yeah? Drop your bomb."

"Can you take it?"

"I mean, I *will*."

"I hope you're ready for this shit because you're getting kidnapped tonight," she says. "I'm your kidnapper."

"Really? You're a kidnapper now?" I laugh. I always laugh when I'm with Lil' Cassidy. She's hard to say no to, but when I'm tired or in a bad mood I have this stupid, self-sabotaging habit of resisting and naysaying people's plans. I know it's happening when it's happening and I know it's bad, but I can't help it—especially on days like this when I've got the self-annihilator in me.

"If you don't pay my ransom—my ransom which is—"

"Which is what?"

"—which is we head on up to the fucking Del Mar fucking

beach house and raid their liquor cabinet and eat all their faaaan-cy-ass muhfuckin' rich-ass bougie food and swim in the pool, maybe find some shit to steal, maybe dig through their jewelry like a coupla Jawas."

I laugh. "You're the worst person on Earth, Lil' Cass."

"I'm the best. Let's dooooo it." She rumbles her fists on the tabletop as she extends the O's in the word "do."

"Now?"

"Now. Right now. Leave your car here. I'll drop you off tomor-row morning or take you to work or you can call in sick or quit or whatever you want. I don't care. Let's just go."

"Is Petra hangin' out?"

Petra Cooper is Cassidy's new girlfriend. When Petra and Cass are together, the night turns into a crazy drug binge. Petra and Cassidy together is too much. It's like hanging out with a cou-ple of daredevils trying to outdo each other. Two Evel Knievels jumping their motorcycles over Grand Canyons all night.

"Petra's got a trig test tomorrow."

"What fun."

"Thanks for the sarcasm, buddy!" says Cass like I'm a toddler. She pats me on the shoulder. "Awww, you did a really great *job*, buddy!"

At Lil' Cassidy's housesitting house we take shots of expensive Japanese whiskey then she demands we make snow angels in the white shag carpet. As we do them, Cass sings, "Santa baby, I want a yacht and really that's not a lot/Santa baby, been an angel all year, Santa baby," and together we sing, "So hurry down the chimney tonight!"

The beach house is really a beach mansion. Everything is white—white marble staircase with gold trim, white marble kitchen counters, white carpets, white stonework fireplace (though unused and spotlessly clean), white-painted high-back chairs (also with gold trim), white satin curtains, white leather sofa in an L-shape with three adjacent loveseats and a Roman fainting couch by the wall of windows facing the dark coastline.

Cass takes me on what she calls "le grand tour." The open front room with the staircase in the center leading to the second-floor bedrooms. First floor—a kitchen bigger than my entire apartment that looks never cooked in, a living room with sunken floors and white shag carpets like polar bear rugs, frosted glass end-tables, mirrors in the hall you half expect to not see yourself in (and it's a surprise when you do). Upstairs—bathrooms like you'd see in pricey restaurants, and in the master a jacuzzi tub with a wall-length mirror behind it. Outside—a heated swimming pool glowing blue in the night, steaming. The pool ends right before the dark cliffside overlooking the sea and beyond that it's inky black, deep night, no moon.

You get the feeling nothing has ever been dirty in this all-white house, and that if it has it's something you don't want to know about, a dirty so foul the knowledge would haunt you. According to Cassidy, the woman who owns this place and lives here with her three teenage daughters, sells art overseas for a living, but there's no art on the walls. Not a bit of color. Color would seem like a stain—red like a splash of blood sprayed out from a slit throat. Pink overtly or perhaps even confrontationally sexual. Green or brown like vast and incorruptible nature creeping up over the white. Color in a place like this would feel like disorder brewing, upsetting the stability of everything white, everything glass, everything pale.

From my tote bag full of stolen office supplies I grab the only cassette I have with me—a mixtape I've made with the first X album on one side and the Locust's record off GSL on the other followed by a few songs from the new Bright Eyes.

After a confusing search for the cassette slot I hit play on the family's crazy entertainment center that's as tall and wide as the wall itself. I turn it up so loud you feel it in the floors—loud enough to hear in the master bathroom upstairs where a few X songs later I buzz Cassidy's head, on orders to leave an eighth inch all around and the scraggly hair in front of her ears like sideburns. This is the haircut she's had for as long as we've known each other, and often I'm her barber. When I cut her hair she calls me "Big Jim." That's my barber name and when I'm Big Jim I'm happier than when I'm regular James. Big Jim is more like Ed—confident yet never arrogant, patient like a country doctor, happy with his own station in life despite adversity. Big Jim isn't assailed with thoughts so awful he has to shake them out of his head like an Etch-a-Sketch, and I mean *physically* shake his head, shake it hard and fast to knock free the words and pictures intruding into his thoughts. Big Jim doesn't want to die and he's not afraid of death. He wants to cut hair and he's fucking good at it.

As I buzz her shining black hair off, singing along with the X song playing downstairs, I stare at us in the mirror—Cass sitting backward on the toilet, arms folded over the top of the tank in her tight black leather jacket with its zippered cuffs (the arms of which are slightly too short for hers), me in my size-small dark blue jean jacket and black t-shirt, a wall of white tile behind us with ornate ivory and silver light fixtures like something from a museum or a movie about drug dealers. We look so serious while we sing along with John Doe and Exene from X. Cassidy's hair drops in thick, black chunks, and we look serious and we look like babies—serious-faced baby-faced babies trying A-for-effort hard to be cool grownups—Cassidy as the shaved head Vietnamese Exene and me as some puny, unhealthy, Slavic John Doe with a bad Spock haircut dyed black. Serious and silly, and we realize it at the same time, and when we realize it, we both laugh just the smallest laugh, and Cassidy says, "Oh god. We're being hopeless romantics again, aren't we?"

I agree, fighting hard to contain my grin which wants to tear my face in half like my mouth is a zipper.

Cass says, "We're such *dorks*. Good thing we're fuckin' *amazing* too."

"Yes," I say factually. "Yes, we are."

"A'ight, Big Jim. You're on hair cleanup duty. Get to it."

"*What?* No, I'm not even—"

"Bitch, don't be a dumb-ass," she says giving me a sour look, "Hopeless romantics don't clean *shit.*"

Back in the big, sprawling, everything-white living room, we flip the tape to the Locust side and crank up the volume and blast it and dance together, holding hands and spinning circles, throwing ourselves around the room, falling down impervious to pain, walking on the furniture, jumping from couch to chair to table to couch again, taking slugs of whiskey from the bottle and sips from something Cassidy calls "the million-dollar gin" then she's tapping out lines of coke on the glass coffee table and cutting them into rows with her fake ID. (Cassidy's just turned 20. Her fake ID is for a 45 year old Chinese woman who stares straight at the camera with a murderous glare.)

"James Jackson Bozic, you terrible disgrace! Do a fucking line with me!" Cass shouts, but she knows I won't. Head down to the table, she plugs one side of her nose with a finger and sniffs in the first line with a rolled-up 20 just as the tape ends. "Oh. This new shit might be garbage," she tells me, saying "garbage" fancy like "gar bawje," then snorts the second line. "Ooh man, actually—" she stands up and plops down on the couch. "This coke is officially trash. Game over. I'm throwing it in the pool." She pats the couch cushion next to her. "Sit with me until I stop dying. If I get a bloody nose you have to jump into action because you're my nurse."

I let myself fall back onto the white couch then reach across to the end-table for the million-dollar gin.

The mixtape ends and the house is quiet.

"Now what?" I say.

"Now what?"

"What do you wanna do?"

Cass sits up straight, excited. "Ooh! The phone!" She grabs it off the table in front of the couch. "Dude, I'm fuckin' calling *Japan*."

"Who do you know in Japan?" I take a sip of the million-dollar gin. It tastes like December, Christmas, a pine forest.

"Japan? No one. It's long distance, dummy. Rack up a big ol' fuckin' bill for Glory Hole."

"Glory Hole" is Cassidy's name for the woman who owns the place, Gloria Hale. She's Glory Hole because, as Cass told me on the drive up here, "She's a mouth-breather and her kinda ugly kinda hot mouth is always open like she wants somebody to shove a snack in there or something. I'm like, 'Hey hey hey,

Glory Hole. I gots somethin' you can shove that hot-ugly mouth down on.'"

"I guess call Japan if you want, but I feel like—I dunno, like she's probably too rich to look at her phone bill. Or—I mean, too rich to be upset by it."

"Oh. Yeah. Probably." Cass sets the phone back on its catch then picks it up again.

"Who you callin' now?"

"Well, it's either Petra or Ghostbusters. I can't decide."

"Tough choice," I say

"That's what I'm here for. Makin' the tough choices. I'm a tough choice maker. Makin' tough choices is my business—"

"—and business is good."

"You got it, babygirl."

Cassidy dials a number. It rings for a while then I hear a muffled voice pick up on the other end of the line and say something I can't make out. "Petra. Hi. No, I'm at the mansion. What? Bein' *rich*. Huh? With James Petra says hi."

"Hi Petra."

"He says hi. Do you want to tell him anything?"

"She doesn't have to tell me anything."

"Petra says you should go punch yourself in the fucking face. Yeah. Yeah, no, I told him. He's walking away."

I go stand at the wall of windows.

The glowing pool below.

The dark sea.

"Cass, let's go swimming," I say over my shoulder.

"James says let's go swimming. Huh? Yeah, you know me. High as fuck. Yeah. Oh, I know. You're just—what was that? Is someone there? Oh. What are you watching? Oh. *Why*? That's stupid.

27

Yeah. Yeah. I know. You sure you can't come over? When? No, I mean tonight. Tonight. What? Tonight. Like now. You can take a break. You can. You—what? Noooo, never."

I stare at the pool and imagine jumping from the window and cannonballing in—hitting the surface with a great upward splash and plunging down to the bottom of the pool, sinking for miles, to the depths of the sea past sharks and treasure chests and shipwrecks, past bubbling thermal vents gushing red gasses, past phosphorescent fish with ugly mouths, down and down and down and down and down and down we go, through the Earth's crust into a lava tube, down, down, to the boiling center of the planet, arms still wrapped around my legs, down, down, down ...

Cassidy and I float in the pool. We hold onto the edge, the heated water steaming in the darkness around us. I close my eyes and kick my feet behind me, just enough to feel my muscles move.

"You tired?" she says quietly, her voice hoarse.

"I'm tired as *shit*. You're not."

"I'm not."

I open my eyes.

The pool glows neon blue in the darkness like a plastic gem, the reflection of the surface swimming in patches of light on the white stucco wall of the pool house.

Along the stone wall bordering the property there are red and blue spotlights the size of soup bowls that shine up from the grass illuminating the palm trees and ferns.

Behind us is the cliff.

Below that, the sea.

You can hear it. The tide is low and there aren't any waves to speak of, but the ocean *hhhish hishhh hhhissshhhhs* down beneath us. *Hhhhisssshhhhs* like a breath gently rising and falling. It's a sound that lulls you off, softens you.

"James, how weird would it be if we were rich like this?"

"I think I'd be a good rich person," I tell her.

"Not me," she says. "I'd be a nightmare like some shitty, evil baron. I'd be a *terror.*"

"You're already a terror."

"What did Dr. Evil tell Mini-Me?"

"You complete me?"

"That."

For a while we say nothing and the silence feels nice.

I think of a pool I swam in as a child in Palm Springs. The desert sky darkening from blue-streaked pink to deep red at dusk. The air so dry it felt alive, and from inside the house the sound of a TV, laughter, applause, a game show.

"You don't have to thank me," Cassidy says after a while, her voice so hoarse now it sounds like she's been lost for years in the same desert I was just thinking of, and the thought of Cassidy emerging from the desert of my childhood shatters my sense of reality.

"I, uh—wait, remind me why I'm thanking you?"

"For this," says Cass. "*This.* This whole place. Isn't it sick?"

"It's pretty sick."

"Bitch, *c'mon*, this place is fucking *dope*. I should *kill* Glory Hole's ass and move in."

I kick away from the side and half-swim half-float toward the deep end.

"Don't drown," says Cassidy. "Think of what your public would say. Think of the community. James! What would the *community* say?!" she shouts, fake-desperate then laughs quietly, pleased with herself.

Treading water in the middle of the pool, out of breath, I say, "If. I drown. You can have. All my—"

"Your what?"

"I'm thinking. You can have—" I try to think of something cool and valuable I have worth leaving when I die, but there's nothing. "If I die you can eat my body."

"*Hells* yeah," she says happily.

I let all the air out of my lungs and sink below the surface.

On the bottom of the pool, eyes closed, I sit cross-legged and feel the smallest push of current moving me—the current from my own body sinking.

All the sound of the world is muffled, blurred to a steady, droning *errrmmm* like machine noise.

And now we shall go away from here.

Sometimes when I want to die I go through the motions of dangerous things.

Driving and veering just slightly to the cliff's edge but not committing to the fall.

Simulated drowning with no chance of drowning because it's harder to drown than you think.

Did Virginia Woolf weigh herself down with river stones?

It helps to be at sea or dropped from a great distance to hit water as hard as concrete.

When I can't hold my breath any longer I kick off the bottom and break through the surface with a gasp.

Tired, my lungs aching and my arms like lead, I swim back to the edge which feels miles away, oceans away, seven seas to swim across.

When I get there Cassidy says, "Let's have a contest to see who can hold their breath the longest underwater."

I belly up over the side of the pool and lie on my back on the cool, dry, rough concrete.

"You suck," she says.

"I need to sleep."

The sky above is black with a gray wash of city light and sea haze.

There are no stars.

"James, sleep is for fools."

"I feel kinda—I dunno—like maybe I'm not actually here."

"James, if you go to sleep I swear to god I'm calling the cops on you."

"Please do. I have their phone number if you want. It's 9-1-1. That's their number."

"I'll tell them you're a serial killer and you've taken me hostage because you want to make a suit out of my skin and they'll come *shoot* your ass."

I tell her I hope she's serious and she laughs and says, "Always, baby."

In a dream I'm drowning in warm, black water. There's a hand gripping my hair and it holds me down as I thrash—holds me down just below the surface and I flail against it and fight to pull away from its grip, but I'm helpless.

I wake up suffocating.

Blind, I smack all around me then Cass takes her thumb and forefinger off my nose and her hand from over my eyes and I gasp hard and lurch straight up in bed.

White walls, shadowy.

Dark wood dresser.

Brass four-poster bed.

Glory Hole's mansion.

Oh. Right.

Cassidy, sitting next to me under the white comforter with a magazine in her lap says "Finally!" and throws the magazine off to the side. "I've been all, 'Jaaames, James, James, *James*' for fucking ever. Let's go. There's a rave at your favorite place Mission Valley."

I drop back and pull the comforter over my face. "Fuck you, Cassidy."

"Get up, you lazy piece of trash."

"Five more minutes."

"No. Let's go. I called Joey Carr—"

"Don't talk to me about Joey Carr."

"—called Joey Carr because I was bored and you were sleeping like a coward, and he was like, 'Oh my gaaawd, Cass. This party. It's so *crazy*. You *have* to come!' Apparently somebody brought a fuckin' nitrous tank and there's free Halloween candy in plastic jack-o'-lanterns everywhere and this guy from Hardkiss is supposed to DJ in like an hour. I actually made coffee already because I'm the boss of all bosses. Close your eyes." I pull the comforter off my face. "Okay, James. Now brrrreathe in like Ferdinand the Bull smmmelling the flowers." I do. "Fuckin' coffee, James. It smells good, right?" I tell her that yes it does in fact smell good then I sit back up in bed and throw the covers to the side.

The building the rave is in is packed with teenagers and older kids my age. After we pay our $20 at the door I lose Cassidy and wander the crowded halls looking for her. The music throbs loud and slow—a steady, rhythmic *oonsk oonsk oonsk* of bass and beats. In the main room the DJ bends low over his turntables, one hand holding his headphones in place, nodding along with the beat.

People dance in some of the dark, red-lit rooms, but mostly they sit on the floor zoned out, eating Halloween candy, sharing bottles of water, playing with neon blue or green or purple glowsticks, giving shoulder rubs, making out, groping under each other's clothes—a hand on a breast under a baggy shirt, hands down the front of jeans, the buttons undone. Bodies and faces, laughing faces, serious faces, shadowy faces. A game of spin-the-bottle is happening in one room, the empty wine bottle slowing to a stop and pointing to a girl who throws her hands over her face in hysterics. I walk past people smoking pot, sucking balloons of nitrous, talking over the music, talking forehead to forehead, talking in each other's ears.

As I walk down the hall looking for Cass, my eyes adjusting to the dark, a blonde girl dressed in a white sports bra and black jeans so wide they look like a dress, grabs me by the hand, pulling me into one of the rooms. Her pupils are like dimes, deep black, her eyes glassy, swimming.

"I know I don't know you but *listen*," she says, and as she talks, I see she has a mini glowstick the size of a match in her mouth. It rolls around her tongue, lighting the roof of her mouth like a ghostly cave. In her arms she cradles an unopened green glass 40 ounce of Mickey's. "Listen," she says again, tucking her thin, straight hair behind her ears with a shaky hand. "Listen. I have—I need to tell you something important. Something big." She's talking very fast and she chews the glowstick between sentences, her jaw tense. "Quick. What's your name?"

"It's, uh—um, it's Ian. Ian Curtis," I tell her, which is what Cass and I do when we talk to weird strangers. Always give a fake name.

"I'm Dana. Now you know me. Good. Okay. Uh, Alan or Ian?"

"Ian."

"Ian, this is really, like, *really* important," she says, handing me the 40 then looking both ways to see if anyone is watching. "Keep this safe for me. I love it—oh god, very, *very* much. I love it more than I could ever explain. Like, to anyone. It's a matter of life and death. Y'good?"

"Yeah, uh, good. I guess?"

"Sweet. Gotta go. Sorry!" she pats my cheeks like I'm a chubby cheeked little kid and before I can reply she's running down the hall, yelling, "Natalie! Nat! Wait up! Naaaaat!"

In each room there are short, squat, black speaker cabinets

linked to the DJ. The further you get from him the quieter the music is until at the end of a hallway I come to a large room full of people talking at normal volume or lying on the ground spacing out, the music barely audible.

On the wall someone has taped up a handwritten sign reading: "Respect the rules of the chill room. PLUR. Peace Love Unity Respect" and underneath the words is a drawing of Bart Simpson with dreads and a Rasta hat smoking a joint while giving the peace sign.

I walk through the crowd and step around people on the floor but no Cass, no Joey Carr, just unfamiliar kids and red-lit darkness, faces, voices, distant music, and—Frances Alicio.

"James!"

Our friend Frances (we call her Frankie) walks toward me, stepping around a kid wearing a white cloth painter's mask, lying down, arms crossed like he's in a coffin, a dark-haired girl in pigtails sitting next to him wearing huge jeans like a mermaid's tail, tapping him on the chest to the muffled beat of the music.

"Frankie! Hey! You're back!"

We hug and she steps away.

"I lost Tyler," she says.

"He's probably dancing."

"Yeah. Tyler," she says laughing. "Is that a fuckin' *40*? Where'd you get a 40 in this place?"

"Some weird girl was like, 'Keep this safe for me' and took off running."

"Can I have a sip?" she asks, which sounds like, "Kive uh sip?"

"Course," I say, passing her the bottle.

Frankie wears a white and brown or maybe black long-sleeved baseball shirt with "A Good Nut is Hard to Find" in letters that are meant to look like rustic wood slats above a smiling cartoon squirrel. She's got on a knee-length skirt that's probably a light color, but you can't see colors in the red light, and she has an Army surplus messenger bag and holds the strap that crosses her chest with both hands as we talk. Her curly, black hair is tied behind her head in an oversized ponytail. She's very pale, but under the red lights she's red like everything else.

"When you get back?" I ask.

"Tonight. Like three hours ago."

"You actually fly?"

"Can you believe it? *Me.*"

Frankie is terrified of flying.

"How was—like, how was Kansas? You wanna go sit somewhere?"

She nods.

I follow Frankie over to the wall which we sit cross-legged against, facing out at the crowd.

"Good spot," I say, setting my tote bag next to me.

"You don't have anything to eat in there, do you?" she asks. "We came straight from the airport."

"It's, uh, it's office supplies from work and random shit like this—" I dig my hand into the bottom and show her a clear glass marble with a swirl of blue and yellow I found in the street a few days ago. "Thought it was kinda cool and—oh, a cough drop. Not exciting."

"Practical, though."

"Here—yeah, here's a pocket knife my grandpa gave me when I was a kid. Couple, like, couple show flyers, old ones, uh, weird little box I found in a parking lot last week. I think it's for a ring. Like a jeweler's box? Oh, check it out—a glowstick I found on the floor."

"Purple. Nice. Another floor find."

"Huh?"

"You pick up stuff you find on the ground. It's a thing."

"Is it?"

"Three of what you've shown me so far has been stuff you've found."

"Oh, I guess I never—I hadn't really thought about it like that but maybe?"

"You do."

"Is it weird?"

"No, no it's not weird."

"I mean, like, *bad weird*."

"No, it's just kinda funny."

"Okay, well, here's this. *Not* off the ground—" I show her my beat-up pocketsize copy of Rimbaud's *A Season in Hell*, the Ed Distler translation I've been carrying for weeks "—and a mix-tape I made. X, Locust, Bright Eyes." I pull the tape out and hand it to her then I show her the stapler I stole from work. "Best of all. Grand finale. Look at this fucking relic."

"Oh nice. Is that super old?"

"I think. It's gotta be. Okay, your turn."

"Show and tell?"

"Shoo und tail," I say in a weird maybe German accent.

Frankie pulls her bag off her shoulder and opens it and begins taking things out and setting them on the floor in front of her.

"Okay," she says, "So, I'll raise you three tapes on your one. Here's the Bright Eyes tape you sent me aaaand we got a mix-tape with Swindle, uh, Submission Hold, Vice Squad, Sake, and Blatz, and *this* one—" She hands me a cassette of Bob Dylan's *Nashville Skyline*.

"Oh cool. I love this record."

"Me too. Then, uh—" she sets the October issue of *Vanity Fair* with Kate Hudson on the cover in front of her. "Bought this at the KC airport for the Sebastian Junger piece on war crimes in

Sierra Leone. And of course my Walkman—" she hands that to me. "And we got *this*—" a Hello Kitty notepad "—with travel notes. Disposable camera. Always have one of those on-hand because you never know what you'll see. Bottle of Dramamine."

"For traveling and swallowing."

"Right, for traveling and swallowing. Also, this—" She sets a little tub of Dr. Pepper flavored Lip Smackers lip balm over Kate Hudson's face on the magazine cover. Oh, and I got this in Kansas right before I left at a gas station." She shows me a bag of Skittles with the end twisted shut.

"Hey, uh, Kansas, was it alright?"

"Kansas was, um—it was okay. It was fine." She begins to re-pack her bag. "Family stuff? Not so good."

"I'm sorry."

"Thanks for the letters and the packages and stuff by the way. That really helped."

"Yeah. Yeah, course. Like, it was—yeah, cool." I want to be articulate and smart around Frankie and I can't because I like her. I like her, but she has a boyfriend even if she won't call him her boyfriend.

"Who you here with?" she asks.

"Lil' Cass. You came with Tyler. Duh. Obviously, because you just said that and—sorry."

A shirtless kid in sagging jeans and a sideways baseball cap walks past saying: "Mitsubishis, Doves, Hearts" to no one in particular, which means he's selling it.

"James, oh my god, why do we *go* to these things?"

"For Tyler and Cass?"

"Yeah, but the music?"

"Sucks."

"It double sucks and these people—I don't know, James. Maybe it's because I've been stuck at my dad's all summer, but these people, I don't want to know *any* of them. You're around people like this and you feel like you're alone. You know what I mean?"

"Oh yeah. Totally." I sip my 40. When I say "Totally" it comes out like "Toe-ahly" and I feel like a moron—a stupid, ignorant beach kid, which is what I am. I want people to think I'm in the Velvet Underground or Joy Division or something dark and cool, but you can't hide the beach. The beach finds its way to the surface no matter how hard you push it down.

"I felt less alone in Kansas at my dad's house, and—I've told you about them—they were drunk half the time they were home. But all these kids? Why are they doing this? What do they want? Who *are* they?"

Because I like Frankie, I have a hard time making eye contact. Staring out into the sea of people is a lot easier.

"*That* kid—" I say pointing at a short guy dancing slowly in a corner to the muffled beat of the music, neon blue glowsticks in his hands, wrists covered in candy bracelets "—he's the son of a doctor in La Jolla, but no one knows his dad is actually selling prescriptions. The kid, Danny—no, David. David Landry. That's his name because that's the name of this kid I went to elementary with that everyone hated and called 'Dirty Laundry.' This guy—he collects Star Wars toys from the new movies and he's super into Jar Jar Binks. Huge Jar Jar fan. The biggest. You should hear his Jar Jar impression. It's almost exquisite. An *exquisite* Jar Jar impression. That was an *exquisite* Jar Jar, my good man."

Frankie laughs. "What about her?" She nods at a frail, dark-skinned girl walking across the room in furry white pants like animal legs and a white bikini top.

"She's—uh, hold on, lemmie think. Animal pants girl. Furry legs. She's, uh—she's a *cop.*"

"No! *Her?*"

"Totally. She's an undercover cop. Like *21 Jump Street* style. Goes to parties and rats people out. She seems like she's rolling when you talk to her, but—but it's an act, she's sober. Oh, and she looks like a kid, but she's actually 30."

"A fuckin' pig. I should've known."

"Yup, a fuckin' pig."

"I like this game," says Frankie.

"Your turn."

"I can't."

"Yeah, you can. Try it."

"That guy—" she says, pointing to a normal-looking kid who's just walked into the room carrying a plastic-wrapped case of water bottles. "He's the promotor's cousin. His name's Kyle. Hates this stuff. Hates this music."

"I like him already," I say. "Kyle, let's be friends. I'm Kyle's best friend now."

"Your best friend Kyle only goes to these things because his cousin caught him—what did he catch him doing?" She looks up at the ceiling and taps her fingers on her knees like she's typing. "Caught him—like, uh, masturbating to animal porn and—"

"Ugh, no. Jesus, Frankie."

"Too far?"

"Maybe. *Maybe.*" I look down at my crossed legs, my sneakers, the concrete floor.

"—and the promotor cousin has made him his slave."

"Harsh," I say, handing her the 40.

"Thanks."

"Yeah."

"So, like, if—if Kyle doesn't do whatever he says, the evil cousin will tell the kid's mom and dad who are, like—they're *gnarly* conversative, fire and brimstone, born-again Christians, and he'll be sent off to military school. In—in *Delaware.* Which is where his best friend—his *last* best friend Max was sent this summer and never came back. Max disappeared one night in the woods behind the school. Word is, um—word is he stumbled onto a drug deal with a bunch of neo-Nazis and they killed him and buried him out in the woods and that people say if you go out into the woods on a night—a night *not unlike tonight* you can see his ghost—you can see ghost Max wandering the moonlit paths looking for a way out. Lost forever in the spooky, mysterious woods of Delaware." She takes a sip and hands the 40 back to me. "That's what happened to Max. Poor Max."

"Good one. We should—"

"Wait. Also—" she continues "—*Also*, Kyle the slave cousin is desperately in love with the undercover cop girl even though they've never spoken. He likes her because she wears those—those big ol' ugly furry animal pants and sometimes bear ears or a raccoon tail. He sees her at parties in her animal clothes and he's afraid to talk to her because everyone knows he's the pro-motor's slave and it kills his self-confidence. Of course, um—of course he doesn't know she's a cop because no one does. He's obsessed with the animal pants cop girl and does everything he can to be around her. He hopes that one night she'll just, like—I dunno, *notice* him and something will click and she'll make the first move because he has absolutely no game at all. They'll run away together somewhere the slave-driving promotor can't find them and they'll just fuck each other's brains out all night and listen to smooth jazz all day and, um—"

"Wait. They like smooth jazz?"

"Furthest thing I could think from techno."

"Oh. Okay. That makes sense. Sorry. Go on."

"They'll fuck each other's brains out and—and they'll listen to smooth jazz and do other non-ravery things like—"

"Take night classes?"

"—and go jogging in the morning and read the classics, read Jane Austen, Henry James, George Eliot, read the Brontës, make all their doctor's appointments for 8am and actually show up, vote for Bush, go fishing, play tennis, play golf, go skiing, go to a chiropractor up in Solana Beach on Fridays, watch ESPN, eat a lot of corn on the cob, eat tons of broccoli, order salads at Sizzler—"

"Whoa, I think you just melted my brain right there. I think I'm in a k-hole. What is reality? What is *time*?"

"K-hole. That's funny. Hey, speaking of Special-K, let's go find Tyler. Wanna go find Tyler?"

"Tyler patrol," I say, standing.

I reach down and help her up.

DESTROY THE RADIO
DESTROY THE RADIO
DEST.ROY THE RADIO!

100.7FM

Tuesday, October 3rd, 2000

Lil' Cass and I leave the rave at dawn and drive around Mission Valley looking for a Mexican place to get breakfast. The streets are foggy. I roll my window down and with the window down you can smell the fog, which is something like wet asphalt and a dusty bookstore. It's a good smell, a smell that makes me feel quiet inside, secure, all the shitty voices of my own stupid suicidal brain pushed down so deep they're only murmurs. I can hear the sound, but I can't make out the words and because of that they have no power over me.

"Glory Hole, you hit me with a flower/you do it every hour," sings Cassidy to the tune of "Vicious," her favorite Lou Reed song. It's a song she sings many times throughout the course of a day, rarely the right way, most often as a parody. Sometimes the lyrics are about how I'm stupid and ugly and a fool, sometimes it's about food or drugs or an interesting dog she'd seen earlier that day.

Sitting in the passenger seat I'm so hungry I feel like my bones are hollow and could snap in two at any moment. To take my mind off it I try to remember all the times Cassidy has sung "Vicious."

In my mind I make a list:

-Sitting on the curb with Cass outside the Golden Hill 7-Eleven on a blazing hot, muggy day in August earlier this year and she's singing "Vicious" with words about hating me because I'm ugly while we share a cherry Slurpee and while cars pull in and out of the parking lot. Sweat drips down my forehead, and I use my arm to wipe it away—the heat of the asphalt baking up through the soles of my sneakers.

-Cass singing "Vicious" with the actual words after doing nitrous in her apartment. I'm sitting on the floor up against the wall with my eyes closed. I'd spent the past hour or so reading magazines, and now in the dark space of my vision I still see the most recent photo I looked at but burned in silver and black negative—Robert Smith from the Cure and Siouxsie Sioux standing next to each other. They're both smiling and Robert's got his hand in a loose fist covering his mouth. Siouxsie is looking at Robert and she has her arm around his shoulders, her hand creeping across the side of his cheek like she's about to grab his face and turn it away from the viewer to look at something off-camera. On her shirt is the mask of a Japanese demon. Robert is wearing black jeans, a paisley long-sleeve shirt, and suspenders. Both are wearing thick eyeliner.

-Cassidy singing "Vicious" last night in the pool with lyrics about doing the dishes. I'm dog paddling laps back and forth to try to sober up and Cassidy stops singing to tell me no more swimming because it's making her feel lazy.

-Cassidy singing "Vicious" last night with the right words while we stand at the bar waiting for our drinks and the bartender tells her she has a nice voice. She says, "Nobody likes a kiss ass" and there's a moment of silence then both she and the bartender laugh and he gives us our drinks free.

-Cassidy singing "Vicious" the real way but in a Miss Piggy voice while we walk through a mall parking lot on the 4th of July looking for her car which we can't for the life of us find. We were at the mall because Cassidy was meant to meet a kid outside AMC-20 who'd promised to sell her a brick of hash. The kid never showed, so we wandered the mall for an hour, looking in the shop windows, judging people's clothing, talking shit, playing the fashion police. For lunch we had soft-baked pretzels in the food court with little plastic tubs of nacho cheese to dip them in. Oh, and lemonade. Good, cold, sweet, bitter lemonade from the pretzel place. Mine, regular. Cassidy's, strawberry.

That's all I've got. I know there are more, but I'm still drunk from last night and my thoughts are drunk thoughts and they race wildly in all directions. They cycle and they stutter as they're led away by another thought sparked in a far corner of my head, and they're chased off by something else I don't have the energy to think about, smacked like a tennis ball in an unexpected direction when I see something outside the window or hear a different song on the radio. As we drive I think of grocery store sheet cake, fireworks, how watermelon candy tastes, and how I never look the same as I think I do when I see myself in a mirror.

Hungry, I think of food. Submarine sandwiches with three kinds of sliced cheese, shredded lettuce, sliced tomato, Italian dressing, salt and pepper, avocado, mayo, mustard, and black olives. Heaping plates of spaghetti with red sauce on top and warm bread on the side. Doritos, Chex Mix, buttered toast, mushroom pizza, everything bagels with cream cheese, refried beans, quesadillas with cheddar cheese puddling out the side, breakfast burritos …

There are no Mexican food places in Mission Valley and its neighboring Fashion Valley is all chain restaurants that aren't open yet and mall parking lots. We drive past office buildings, industrial block warehouses passing like white container ships in the fog, gray concrete and gray sky, damp palm trees, American flags limp above California bear flags hanging just as lifeless, and eucalyptus trees standing high above everything.

It's fall only you can't tell. Fall looks like winter which looks like spring which looks like summer.

I pull the sun visor down and stare at my face in the mirror— bloodshot eyes with the blue blasted out so far they're nearly colorless and those ever-present dark circles.

Ugh, is what my thoughts say when I see myself.

Ugh.

Cassidy and I drive to Golden Hill because we know Humberto's will be open and because the thought of their breakfast burritos is now the only thing keeping me alive.

While we wait for our food at a table by the window, cars passing by slow in the gray morning, Cassidy licks the tip of her pinky finger then dips it into a little bag of coke the size of a credit card she keeps in the inside pocket of her leather jacket and rubs it against her gums.

"I can't *believe* you sometimes," I tell her.

"What? What can't you believe?"

"*You.* You're gonna get caught some day, Cass."

She sings, "You're gonna get caught/just you wait and see," then before the "why's everybody always picking on me?" part of the song she says, "Caught doing what?"

"Being you. Being insane."

"If I'm crazy then I'm glad," she says.

"What does that mean?"

"I don't know. Look, James, I want to give you a special award now for rallying like a muhfucker and having fun at the party." (Our friends call raves "parties" most of the time.)

"What kind of award do I get?"

"A wonderful award for a wonderful, special boy."

"What do I win? A car?"

"A trophy."

"I don't want it."

"Your trophy says—on the front of the trophy it says in gold letters—" she clears her throat for emphasis, then adopts a posh English accent like the Queen, "Squire James Jackson Bozic, thank you for your service in rallying like a mother ahem *fucker* and having fun at the party."

"I'm a squire? Why not a sir?"

"You gotta earn that shit, baby. Uh, man, wow—I can't believe how wack that E was Joey had."

"Probably baby aspirin," I tell her.

"Joey wouldn't play me like that."

"Joey's ruthless."

"Joey has no Ruth?"

"None," I say. "Not even one Ruth. Not even a tiny one the size of a little doll."

"Is Ruth short for something?"

"The name?"

"Yeah," she says. "The name. What's it short for?"

"Besides Ruthless? I don't know. I think Ruth is just Ruth."

"How sad. Hey, I saw you talking to Frankie. She's back, huh? Well, obviously, right. No duh. When she get back?"

"She flew in last night."

"Kansas sucked?" Cassidy screws the lid off the thermos and takes a sip. "I can't believe this is still *warm*. I'm the king of coffee. Bow down before your king, you shitty fools."

"No, Kansas was fine. Stuff between her and her dad and step-mom sucked."

All summer I wrote emails back and forth with Frankie in Kansas. Frankie—bored, drinking too much at dinner even though she's only 19, reading all the World War II books in the basement library, listening to the Bright Eyes mixtape I sent her. Me—bored at the internet newspaper writing to her about our press junket to the Del Mar Fair where the staff photographer took photos of me riding the rides after which I'd "review" the rides in my notebook to post on the site later. Frankie emailed about the Army base in town and Kansas women with dramatic, feathery mullets and toilet bowl planters as yard art. I wrote about Lil' Cass and Petra and I driving to the desert so they could do mushrooms and how Petra decided her holy mission was to move to New York City so she could assassinate the cast of *Friends* and how once that happened "the shitty timeline we're in that began with Shannon Hoon from Blind Melon's death would go back to normal." Frankie—letters about red wine hangovers, her dad and stepmom's patriotically-named housecat Liberty they brought back from Saudi Arabia, discourse on Hole's *Celebrity Skin*, quiet nights AIMing her boyfriend-not-boyfriend, wanting to cut herself because she knew she would feel better afterward. Me—emails about sitting on the hood of my car in beach parking lots at dusk, the sunset like a postcard while Cass buys drugs in the public restroom. Long emails. Pages. Pages while AJ sitting cross-legged under his desk tells Emily about the endless group of guys he's fucking. Pages written while Emily talks to AJ about working at Faque Burger in the '90s and about her all-time favorite blowjob she's given. Pages telling Frankie all the best Lil' Cassidy stories, her relentless acquisition of cocaine and speed, Cassidy's theories about certain Cure songs mirroring the structure in *The Divine Comedy*, and things she's learning about Vietnam from her dying aunt who wants to tell her everything she knows before she's gone. Long emails typed in the office to get me from 9am to 5pm. Long emails to show off my writing in ways I realize are obvious and embarrassing upon rereading them—me ripping off Lester Bangs or ripping off Patti Smith or Claude Bessy or Jim Carroll. An insufferable poetic description of chewing sour grass while sitting on a warm, dusty, gum-marked sidewalk in Ocean Beach while the clouds race overhead like gray battleships. A fake Hemingway passage about standing on the shore watching the sea in the afternoon.

The long emails got me through a summer of work days, and sitting in the taco shop across from Cassidy waiting for our breakfast burritos I know as soon as she drops me off I'll start one to Frankie about the cats on the internet meeting yesterday and Glory Hole's Del Mar beach mansion last night, about how badly I wanted to die and how it's still there though I'm trying my best to ignore it, how I push it away by drinking, staying awake too long, going places at all hours of the night and day, acting wilder than I feel, never going home, talking without cease to friends so as not to think, emailing her (Frankie) to keep from being quiet with myself. None of this I told her last night at the rave. I can type it, but I can't say it.

I pull my rolling chair out and sit down at the u-shaped cubical I share with AJ and Emily, who are in front of their computers, headphones on, typing. Emily, her frizzy red hair pulled back into stubby, thick twin braids today, picks up her coffee without looking at it, blows on it, then takes a careful sip. AJ writes and sends one brief email after another. A few words for each. A line. Maybe two. I can't tell what he's doing, but whatever it is he's on rapid fire. Type, type, type, send. Type, type, type, send.

While my iMac powers up I put on headphones, and open the disc drive on the computer tower under the desk. In goes the Locust's three-inch mini-CD and the tray retracts automatically.

It takes ages for the computer to start so I pull off my headphones, get up, and walk down the hallway that leads to the breakroom. The carpet is dark blue with little triangle flecks of orange in a manic pattern along with fat, stubby lines of white like small noodles. Stare at it too long and you get dizzy. You get dizzy and you start to feel the world tip and your knees wobble like you're walking on the deck of a ship at sea. Being at work drunk with this carpet is a whole new level of seasick so I walk straight, stare straight ahead.

The breakroom has a square, orange formica table in the middle hardly anyone sits at with a metal box that holds napkins, a white plastic salt shaker next to a black plastic pepper shaker, and a bottle of Tabasco Brendan keeps in here for the Taco Bell Burrito Supremes he lives off. Lining the walls are gray metal cabinets kept empty except for spare rolls of paper towels, a box of straws that's never been opened, and a case of extra napkins. Below the cabinet nearest the door sits the microwave and next to the microwave is the Mr. Coffee, which is always full thanks to Monica the receptionist. The coffee is terrible. It's thin and bitter but the wrong kind of bitter.

Next to the coffeepot is a pink cardboard box of C&H sugar, a red and orange plastic cannister of Coffee Mate powdered creamer, and a row of shiny black mugs with the newspaper's name on them in a red-trimmed white font that's almost Old English though not as hard to read.

I grab one of the cups, check it first for dust inside, then take the coffee pot from its hot plate, and pour myself a cup.

Next it's sugar to kill the taste.

I hold the box of C&H high above the cup like I'm a world-class bartender.

As the sugar pours into my cup, I hear someone walk in behind me.

I turn and it's Amir from tech support.

Amir does something that involves getting rid of computer viruses. He's in our department often. Fixing problems. Saving the day.

"Hello James, my friend," he says sitting down at the table with a Tupperware container and a plastic fork. Amir is the only person I've seen use the table besides the maintenance guys. "Your sugar, it is too much. Too much for you, my friend."

"I know. But this coffee?"

"Yes. This coffee, it is shit," he laughs. Amir rarely swears but when he does he laughs and when he laughs you laugh.

"I'm also—" I lower my voice "—uh, still—*drunk* from last night. Don't tell anyone."

"Oh, you bad, *bad* boy," he says happily. "They are going to throw you out of this place. You want to try?" He shows me his food. It's some kind of rice dish. White rice with green herbs chopped up in it.

I sit down at the table across from him and he slides the Tupperware to me with his white plastic fork stabbed into the middle of the rice like a harpoon.

"Cool if I use your fork?"

"Of course, my friend. This is Ifra's mother's rice recipe. Iranian food. Is very good. You will like a lot and if you don't I will throw you out the door." Amir likes to joke about throwing people out of things. When you're not feeling amazing it's nice to be around people who like to joke. Especially when your way of coping with not feeling amazing is to joke.

The rice is buttery and you can taste garlic, green onions, cilantro, and parsley. "Amir, this is great. Tell Ifra it's great."

"She knows, my friend, she knows. Ifra, she is not insecure. She act like she is Napoleon." Amir slides the tips of his fingers into the gap in his spotlessly white oxford shirt like Napoleon. "When she is too much I tell Ifra, 'Do not invade Russia in the winter please' and she say, 'Fuck you, Amir.'" He laughs and then I'm laughing.

"Hey, uh—thanks for the snack."

I slide the Tupperware back across the table, but he waves both hands in front of him and says, "No, no, have. *Have.* I am always getting this food. For you, maybe it is different."

I eat more and we talk. I tell him about last night. Cassidy's housesitting job at the Del Mar mansion. The pool on the cliffside. The rave.

While I talk about the breakfast burritos Cass and I got earlier at Humberto's, Amir gets up and walks over to the set of vending machines behind us.

"James. Cheez-Its. They are good?"

"Amir, *what*? You've never had *Cheez-Its*?"

"I have never."

"Holy shit. Cheez-Its are the king of all snacks. You gotta get Cheez-Its."

"I will take your word, my friend."

"Take it. My word is yours."

Amir plunks three quarters into the slot, taps in the code, and the red and orange mini bag of Cheez-Its drops into the tray.

Back at our cubicle my computer hasn't finished booting up. Across the black screen runs lines of pale gray code, silent, endless. Emily and AJ peck away at their keyboards and the news guys over in their corner are talking about William Shatner. They call Shatner "Bill" and Bill Shatner is an honorary member of their news department Bill club. They like Bill Shatner ironically and it's become an inside joke to talk about him as often as they can. Older guy irony is softer than young person irony, but it's still irony and their devotion to the endless joke is admirable.

"Bill Shatner was so bloated on *Rescue 911* last night it was like there were other Bill Shatners inside him," I hear Chris Yates say.

"Like a Russian nesting doll, Bill?" asks Bill Cerone.

"Yeah, Bill. Like a series of bloated, grinning, beady-eyed Bill Shatners and each one smaller than the rest until the smallest Bill Shatner you can't even see with the naked eye."

"That's cute, Bill."

Finally my computer screen comes to life and the desktop loads the icons for our email, Recycle Bin, Internet Explorer, Microsoft Word, and Xtrem, the back-end program we use to build the site. AJ likes to say "Xtrem" in a stoned bro California accent. "Brah, Xtrem is *xtremly* fuckin' slow today." (Sometimes he does it in a Cartman from *South Park* voice, which is nearly the same, just faster and higher pitched. Both make Emily furious, but AJ loves that it pisses her off, and knowing Emily I'm sure she likes to hate it too.) In our department we use Xtrem to create the event profiles for the entertainment sections we manage—SD Arts, Live Music, Film Scene, Classical San Diego, Bars & Nightlife, Out of Towners, Sports and Lifestyle, Kidz Eventz, Literary and Library, and Eats.

First I open Internet Explorer, type in www.hotmail.com, and check my personal email. I find ads, spam about prescription drugs, bank statements, a tour announcement for a band I used to like, and a message from giant.cassidy.nguyen@raveworld. net with the subject: "you wheel die soon" and the body text "meet me at the #&%@ing shay kaffay tonight or you'll seal yr own fate. YOU HAVE BEEN WARNED, DUMB $#!&!" All of which I delete.

Next to my keyboard, to the right of my mousepad, I've got a list Ed printed out of all the events happening this week. It's held in place with a black and silver binder clip and it's thick like a magazine. This is what I do each day—hours spent going through the list, the list that never ends. Once I finish putting in an event, I trace over it with a highlighter and move on to the next listing. When the list is done, Ed gives me a new one.

The first event is a show on October 24th with the Foo Fighters, Queens of the Stone Age, and Slobot. I open Xtrem and click "Add" at the top of the dark gray page with its sections arranged in rectangular blocks of lighter gray. I type the location, date, time, cover, and band names into their respective fields. In the middle of the page is a white square for the event write-up. Usually we write the profiles in Word then paste them into the field. When it's a show I don't care about I just type into the field and go. Keep it short and dry. Get info from the PR one-sheet bio they mail out along with the band's newest CD or hit up AllMusic.com or the CMJ site. I'll say something about the headliner's new record if there is one, type in <I></I> HTML code for italics on the album title and <P></P> code for the paragraphs. I'll mention anything the venue's website says about the show—maybe there's a special guest that's not been announced yet; maybe an event will have a food sponsorship, free tacos or a barbeque stand or dollar shots. If we've written about them before I'll link to the older piece with <a href=" then whatever the link is, followed by a "> and after that the text that will stand in for the link then </a> as a closer.

If it's a band I hate, I say that I hate it without saying "I" or "hate," and I try to be as mean as possible. That's something new. When I first got the job earlier this year I was afraid of being fired. For a very brief moment I thought I might have a career ahead in journalism. I figured maybe if I worked hard enough and played my cards right I might make an honest go of it. I could build my resume, save up money, move to a bigger paper or a magazine, maybe *The Village Voice, Rolling Stone, Interview, The New Yorker.* I'd pay my rent and utilities on time each month then after a few years I'd buy a house and I'd get a car I could count on to start every morning. In this fantasy I would have nice things—a wine cellar, good clothes, an expensive pair of the eight hole Doc Martens my parents wouldn't let me wear in high school, and a library of books, yes, a wall of books in front of my writing desk. I'd be a collector. All of Proust. All of Dickens. First editions of Didion's *White Album* hoarded like a dragon does gold. Broadsheets. Galleys. Signed copies of *The Bell Jar.* A whole row of them.

At this point I know I'm not a journalist and that what we're doing in our department isn't journalism anyway. Except on the rare days the news guys need me run out and cover something they don't have time to do, what I'm writing for the paper isn't worth fussing about. Ed doesn't care what I write as long as I get the list done on time. He knows I'm young and that a lot of people like whatever young people do even if it isn't great, and after my name showed up as one of the regular search results in our monthly site diagnostic, he let me have free rein.

I've been pushing it lately. Robert Wyland, a painter who does these awful, perfect, shitty sea life paintings got a write-up where I listed all the things better than him that also start with the letter W. It was a fuck you both to Wyland and to the kind of coverage we do here at the paper. Better than Robert Wyland? The list ran seven paragraphs long. Wizards, witches, wands, walls, Williams, Wimbledon, Wednesdays, Willy Wonka, wicks, wood, and on and on. It was the stupidest, most obnoxious bullshit ever and no one cared. Part of me *wanted* to be told no, *wanted* to get shut down. But nothing.

Another event profile last week was for a Christian emo band my friends and I love to talk shit about. I wrote it as a one-act play with made-up dialogue between Cass and Tyler. The play showed the two of them walking from Ranchos at 30th Street and University in North Park to the Warsaw goth night at the

Empire Club discussing all the different ways they wanted the lead singer to be killed. Still no one here said a thing. All my fictional Tyler and fictional Cassidy's talk of beheading and evisceration passed right under the radar.

When the event is something I like it's generally not on the list Ed gives me. Those events I add in because I want people to go. Shows at the Ché Café, at the Casbah, World Beat Center, the Ken Club, the Livewire, Scolari's Office, the Mira Mesa Epicentre, bars like Tilly's down in Tijuana, a rare show at SOMA or upstairs at Gelato Vero, event spaces rented out for the night, or the occasional house party where the organizers are cool with having the location listed.

I type all the info for the Foo Fighters show, then I remember my Locust CD is cued-up.

Headphones back on.

Volume loud.

And type.

Not write.

Type.

Emily and AJ and I go out for lunch at Pokéz in Downtown after an all-staff meeting about Halloween ad content. Pokéz is a hip Mexican restaurant everyone I know loves except AJ who only likes McDonald's and pizza. AJ comes along for the ride because he's in hopeless, unrequited love with one of the waiters, who (according to AJ) is "so straight he'd walk into a wall rather than turn a corner."

AJ's a smart, antsy, dark-eyed, high-strung guy who grew up in New Jersey and moved out here the summer after college. He wears the same ratty camel hair coat every day. Baggy chinos or dockers. A button-up shirt he doesn't tuck in, sometimes a t-shirt if he's too hungover to care. But the coat, every day the coat, no matter the weather. AJ knows he's different in a very polarizing way and he likes it, cultivates it, never combs his curly dark blonde hair that stands up unruly, his beard the same, short but a mess. He wears beat-up old creepers from his high school goth days or stylish dress shoes with the buckle on top. He's very careful about his look. We all are. Me, Emily, Cass, Frankie, Tyler, Joey Carr. But AJ even more so because his look is a hard one to pull off. It exists somewhere between Mafia wise-guy and paranoid shut-in who can't handle society but is very well read. AJ looks like Zeus—leonine, Saturnine, a shorter Zeus, short but stocky. Everything about him makes you think he's a big guy, but he's five eight in heeled shoes. AJ's got a personality as tall as the sky, the kind of presence that either fills up a room and draws everyone to him, or weirds people out and shoves them away. He's happy with either outcome (and probably more so the latter). AJ talks fast. Talks a lot. And now he's in the front passenger seat while Emily drives, entertaining her with the list of guys (and one girl) he's seeing. That's an AJ thing. He's a kisser and a teller—the least discrete person on Earth.

I'm sitting in the back, listening, bored, hating myself for drinking so much last night. I'm not drunk anymore. Just hungover. It's one of those hangovers that never ends unless you sleep it off or start drinking again. At Pokéz I'll get a couple bottles of Modelo Negra and hit up AJ for his flask of tequila with my food and that'll help knock it out. Hair of the dog—hair and the collar and fangs and claws and everything else right down to the fleas.

To take my mind off how I feel I pull the Distler translation of Rimbaud out of my tote bag and open it to a random page and read:

"I became master of the simple hallucination. In place of an abattoir I now saw a mosque, a team of drummers led by archangels, carriages flying the interstates of the sky, a dim-lit drawing-room at the bottom of a lake; demons, phantoms of a cadaver's past; the title of a melodrama would lift terror before me."

We idle in traffic getting into Downtown while AJ describes "the Tattooed Lawyer." None of the people have names in AJ's stories. Just codes. "The Dirty Talker." "Hot Skater Guy," also referred to as "Femme Tony Hawk." "Mean Business Lady" is the girl he's seeing. "The Arrogant Surfer" was last week. Codes. So maybe he is discrete in his own way. Still, it's a lot, and it's more than a lot when you're hungover.

Emily is desperately, painfully in love with AJ. She's just as candid as he is and loves to shock people with her own sex stories. Emily dresses more like me—tight jeans, too-small denim jacket, t-shirt, band pins, Converse. We're from the same scene. She's older than me (both her and AJ turned 30 this year), but we know the same people, love the same bands, read the same writers (though Emily's more into the continental Europeans where I tend toward American authors. She likes Zola, Raoul Vaneigem, Anatole France, Kafka, Balzac. My copy of the Distler Rimbaud translation was a gift from her). Today, although she's dressed like everyone in our scene, the formula has changed. It's become cleaner this fall, more 1950s teen delinquent by way of John Waters than turn-of-the-century punk like before. Most of our friends wear jeans, sneakers. Denim jackets, hoodies, and pea-coats are hip right now. This is how Emily has dressed since I've known her, but today her jeans are red, blood red, her new denim jacket white as a cloud. The button-up shirt she wears is lace and silk, something Victorian, as pale white as her skin, jeans as red as her hair.

Our friends dress so alike it's embarrassing sometimes. I'm dressed just like Emily but mine is blue denim. My black and white Converse sneakers are dirty, beat to hell. The formula has changed for Emily—just slightly yet drastic in its own way. Sometimes reinvention is about one seemingly insignificant element of an equation swapped for another. Emily's look is wildly different through subtle revisions and variations. Next to Emily I look like a stray dog. Next to AJ, who is also a dog, I'm a lost puppy—ugly, a mutt, while AJ is a fighting breed, not pure but mercurial, rough, important. On the surface Emily is the opposite of swarthy, heavy, slovenly AJ. She's tall, slight, has death-white skin, deep-set green eyes ringed in heavy black eyeliner, dark red hair in tight frizzy curls like Poison Ivy from the Cramps. (To say AJ and Emily are "cooler" than me would both be correct and missing out on the multi-faceted complexity of how far out of my league I am when we're together. I'm not a burden, but I'm definitely a "kid" to them.)

Aside from the physical, and betraying outward appearances, Emily and AJ are more alike than you might think. They're industrious, decadent, mean sometimes but mean in order to be funny for the most part. They're also pretentious, careless, self-destructive, and unaware. AJ and Emily would be an ill-fit couple but also perfect. If the 5 percent of AJ that likes girls ever lines up with the 100 percent of Emily who lives for him, the combination would be incandescent. They're both full of shit in so many ways, but their driven, ambitious, over-the-top sense of delusion gives them an air of the superhuman.

AJ is talking. AJ is always talking. He says (to Emily, driving), "So, the fuckin' Tattooed Lawyer came over last night."

"Oh *yeah*?"

"Yup. We got a pizza delivered from Mazara's. Did some shots. Smoked some weed. Watched a lil' b-ball."

"Which one is b-ball?" asks Emily.

"Which one?"

"Which game."

"Oh, it's baseball," he says.

I unbuckle my safety belt and lean into the front between the two seats and say, "B-ball is basketball," then sit back down.

"How do *you* know that, Mr. Art Kid?" asks AJ looking at me in the rearview.

"Common human knowledge."

"Well, we watched baseball," says AJ, resuming his story. "Not b-ball."

"You *hate* baseball!" says Emily who knows everything there is to know about AJ.

"Ehhh, y'know, baseball I could take or leave," he holds his left hand out in front of him and tips it side to side to show ambivalence.

"Shut up. You know you hate it."

"I do. But the Tattooed Lawyer? He's into it and maybe I might get into it too. You know, interest by association."

"Until you *fuck* the Tattooed Lawyer and forget all about it," she says wickedly.

"Oh, don't get me *wrong*. I *fucked* the Tattooed Lawyer. Last night. Checked *that* particular box. But this is not a one-time thing. Me and him? We click." He snaps his fingers. "We click like crazy." When he says, "crazy" he points a finger at his left temple and twirls it around in a circle. "We click like a fuckin' train. Clickety clack."

"How was he?" Emily loves hearing details about what AJ does in bed.

"He's tattooed all over. The Illustrated Man. Tattoos on his feet. On the bottoms of his feet. Imagine how that would feel."

"How many times?"

"How many times we fuck?"

"Yeah. How many?"

"Twice. I, uh—we wanted to keep going. I mean, you always want to keep going, right? But we were pretty drunk and kinda high and I'd done a little blow earlier so y'know." His voice makes a shrugging sound without him actually shrugging.

"He spit or swallow?"

"Spat."

"Lame."

AJ laughs. "He's cool. I'm seeing him again tonight. Going to Bar Dynamite."

"Lame," says Emily again.

"It's his scene. He's into DJs. Knows a bunch of them. Likes going to see them wherever they are."

"Lame."

I roll down my window and the fresh air feels good on my face. Downtown is gray. Shades of gray. Faded stucco and old concrete. Taller buildings blocking out the light as we pass, shading the streets. Warehouses with black plastic trash bags out front. A thrift shop with Halloween decorations in the window. A rough bar with men smoking in a group by the open door, the bouncer sitting on a chair under the awning hunched over a Chinese take-out container. We pass dumpsters, tagged-up walls, chain-link fences, a homeless camp with tents and shopping carts, and a man on his knees rolling up a sleeping bag while a dog stands watching him. I open the Rimbaud again and read: "Once, if the specter of memory serves me true, the life I lived was a banquet and wild feast where each heart was revealed beating and where wine flowed like dark rivers."

We're stuck in traffic a few blocks from the restaurant and AJ and Emily are talking about the guy she hooked up with last night.

"*Dude,* he was *so* bad at everything," she says. "So bad. Nothing was good."

"Something had to be good," says AJ. "Something's always good."

"Making out—pretty good. We kissed for a long time on my couch and I began to—I was like, is this guy *ever* gonna fuck me? I was *ready.* It was like—I kept waiting for him to do something and—like, man, I was *very* wet. Finally, when *I* took off my jeans, he went down on me, and he couldn't keep a rhythm. It was terrible. It was like free jazz. No structure. No direction. When we finally fucked he came in like a minute. No joke. Like 60 seconds. Squirt, squirt, *done.*"

"Yeaaah, amateur hour," says AJ sadly or maybe just tired, staring at the buildings passing. He holds his hand out the window and lets it coast on the breeze like a seagull.

"Amateur *minute,*" says Emily, followed by a mean, short laugh. "He was, all, 'I'm gonna come, I'm gonna come!' and I'm like, 'Dude. Not yet. Slow the fuck down!' because I wasn't even *close.* I hadn't even started touching myself yet. Then he pulled out and tried to get the condom off so he could finish on me. He kept saying, 'I'm gonna come on your fucking tits!" over and over again, but he just jizzed inside the condom before he could peal it off. Ugh, yeah—I don't know, maybe that was like a blessing in disguise or something because you don't want that kinda guy's cum on you. Yeah, keep that shit in the condom, bro."

"Carnival of errors," says AJ in a French accent. *Carny vall of eh roars.* "Can I use 'amateur minute' in a story?"

"You have my permission," she says.

"Maybe that'll be the title. Amateur Minute. It's genius, Emily."

"You should write about how after he came—ugh, this is so lame—the guy lay next to me and cried for—AJ, I'm not even kidding—five straight minutes. Five minutes is a long time to cry. It doesn't sound like that much, but when you—when you actually *witness* that shit firsthand? Holy fuck, it's a lot. I laid there and watched the—like, the numbers on the clock radio and listened to him cry and—ugh, *so* awkward. He kept apologizing, 'I'm so sorry, Emily. I can't believe it. I'm sorry, sorry, sorry,' then he tried to go down on me again and I pulled him back up, like, nnnnnope, not happening."

"Pathetic."

"Me or him?"

"Him. Jesus, Emily. *Him.*"

"I was gonna *say.*"

"I dunno, Emily. Maybe a dipshit like that doesn't deserve a story. Even a story that's mean to him. Posterity hath no room for Amateur Minute. I might use the part about 'you don't want that kinda guy's cum on you' because that's brilliant. You're on a roll today, honey."

"It's all yours," she says.

"Thanks. You know I appreciate it." He takes his sunglasses off and rubs them on the front of his shirt then says, "My, uh—my eventual posthumous glory will celebrate your generosity."

"It better."

"You and me, honey, up in the stars."

AJ and Emily are the best writers on staff. Emily writes nothing except journalism and only for the paper. She has no interest in fiction or anything beyond what she writes at work. Her plan is to rise within the organization, get promoted, take over as editor one day. All her energies (which are substantial) are focused in that direction.

AJ can write whatever—news copy when he's asked, arts stuff, human interest, election coverage, business section profiles, whatever Ed throws at him, but he can also hold his own writing fiction. AJ drinks around the clock and does more drugs than anyone I've ever met, but a couple years ago when he wasn't getting wasted every night, he wrote half a novel. I'd heard him and Emily talk about his book a few times, so last week I asked to read it and he emailed me the file, subject-line: "i don't fucking know."

AJ's novel (the half he finished) is about a man living in an un-named European city during Nazi occupation. The man does what he can to hide his Jewish neighbor and eventually the two men fall in love. Neither character is given a name. The man is "the Man" and his neighbor is "the Neighbor" and the Neighbor lives in a cramped back room hidden behind a bookcase. They see each other at night and talk in letters shoved through the space between the bookcase and wall.

The letters are in the book, and they give the story an urgent, breathless sort of realism paired with immediacy that sweeps you up along with it. You understand why the Man loves the Neighbor and why the Neighbor loves him and why the Man would do anything to keep him alive.

When the Neighbor tells the Man the story of his family's murder it's devastating. He tells how it happened, and they make love for the first time, and in the morning what's left of the town's Jewish population is loaded onto trucks and taken to the train station to be shipped to the camps.

That's where it takes a strange turn. The Jews board the train. The doors of the boxcars are pulled shut then locked—locked like a cattle car full of cows bound for slaughter. Slowly the train picks up momentum and chugs a mile down the snowy track when suddenly all the passengers vanish.

At the first stop, the bleak white fields of snow all around and the dark woods in the distance, the guards go back to check on them and there's no one, nothing, empty train cars, not even a solitary shoe left behind.

In the next chapter all the people on the train show up in modern day New York City. They appear out of nowhere in a big group in the middle of a Manhattan intersection with their old-fashioned coats and hats and suitcases, and that's where AJ stopped writing. After that scene, a few lines down the page, is the last thing AJ typed, a single question mark.

Like this:

?

We park a couple blocks from Pokéz and AJ and Emily walk ahead of me down the street sharing a cigarette. AJ tells Emily about the girl he dated before he realized he liked men better. "Her name was Erikah," he says, "and she called herself 'Erika with an H' and so did everyone else. She was cool. Worked at Entertainment Exchange. Played in a bunch of bands. I feel bad about how it ended."

"How'd it end?" asks Emily.

"Bad," says AJ.

As we get closer I see Frankie and a couple guys I don't recognize standing outside Pokéz next to a wall-length mural on the side of the building. It looks like they're saying goodbye. Hugging. One of the guys (a short one) jumps up in the air and high-fives the other (a tall one) and they turn and walk around the corner leaving Frankie standing alone.

AJ and Emily go in the restaurant while I stay outside with Frankie. We talk about how boring the rave was last night and how boring all raves are and why do we ever go to those fucking things and why are we always asking each other why we go to those things, why don't we just *not*? Both Frankie and I are wearing our clothes from last night and we talk about that too, about not going home, about staying up all night and how tired we are now but the day has begun and oh I guess we'll stick it out because what else are we going to do?

For a while we stop talking while Frankie lights a cigarette. We stand next to each other and watch the traffic pass—the endless procession of cars traveling up E Street, a city bus stopping for the light with a hiss of brakes, a Japanese motorcycle and the man riding it is wearing a helmet painted like a jack-o'-lantern. We talk about how there's no fucking way he can see out of that and we talk about how Tyler's made a batch of speed in the chemistry lab at his school and wants everyone to try it and how I'm afraid he's going to fuck up and lose his scholarship. Frankie assures me he won't. She says Tyler's always understood exactly what to do and what not to, how the whole time they've known each other he's been on a steady path. I tell her I have no path at all except wanting to write (which sounds dorky and immature as soon as I say it) and she tells me she's thinking of dropping out of Mesa and might like to do something in the arts as well. Maybe photography. I ask her if she has a good camera and she tells me she doesn't and that she's got no money at the moment, but she has an old checkbook from a closed bank account and is thinking of going to Target to write a bad check and get the best camera she can find. I tell her it's a great idea and that I'll go with her and stick the place up if anyone gets wise to the plan. She likes the stick the place up idea and tells me to bring as many weapons as I can find and I tell her I can find *a lot* of weapons, don't even worry about that. I ask her if she wants to have lunch with me ("with me and AJ and Emily?") but she says something like I can't, sorry, I wish, and she looks at her watch and it's the first time I've noticed her with a watch and I realize at that moment it's the first time I've seen her smoke a cigarette, so maybe things are changing. Frankie says her boyfriend is meeting her at a coffeeshop only she doesn't say boyfriend, she says his name, but she says it in a way that feels like he's her real boyfriend now, like maybe something unspoken has been confirmed or acknowledged or substantiated. I tell her I'm going in now, but by the time we hug goodbye and I turn to head inside, AJ and Emily are walking out, white to-go boxes in hand.

AJ and Emily drop me off at the Livewire after lunch so I can get my car, and I take the long way back to the office to kill time. I drive and listen to the Bright Eyes section of my mixtape and watch the liquor stores and restaurants and bars roll past. I drive down sunny streets with canvas awnings, palm trees along the sidewalk, fire hydrants, parked cars, mailboxes, telephone poles. University Heights to Hillcrest then a quick detour into Mission Hills to see the old Craftsman cottages before hitting the freeway, at which point the X side of the mixtape begins and I drive and shout the lyrics, windows down, air (warm and dry) buffeting wild through the cab and drowning out the music and my voice until I sing along from memory.

Back at the office I do the mail scam I figured out my first week here—package up whatever you want to send and take it to Monica the receptionist and she'll mail it off for you. It's assumed that whatever you need delivered will be official work business.

When Frankie was out in Kansas I sent letters, CDs, mixtapes. Friends across the country get care packages—books, magazines, elaborate promo packs we're given for movies and art shows. Every few days I write to my grandparents in Arizona. My grandpa Cecil will write back, but usually it's my grandma Drusilla who replies. I send letters, drawings, photos, and sometimes cowboy novels I pick up in thrift stores, and they send back postcards from the places they've lived—Bullhead City in Arizona, La Veta, Colorado, Grants Pass on the California Oregon border, and now Lake Havasu City where they rent a spot in a trailerpark in the desert overlooking the lakeshore.

My childhood memories of visiting them are the best things I've got. You can't put your memories in a will or in a safe deposit box or a time capsule for the future. You lose them when you are gone, and because they were yours and no one else's, they are irretrievable—unless you write them down. If you write what you remember you can make it live again—you can save what you love from oblivion, or at least delay its eventual descent. I think of these things often—the grassy, quiet plateau behind their farmhouse in La Veta with horses eating clover along the fence-line and the Sangre de Cristo mountains blue and dim in the Colorado haze. My grandpa's western spirit and gentle heart. My grandmother's sarcasm, which is dry but soft and never cutting, less a thing of judgement than wit and good humor. I think of reading picture books about tractors under the dining room table while my grandparents drink coffee and talk about cattle or plan a trip to town for groceries and farm supplies. With the sea so far away it felt like a dream.

Today I write my grandparents a short letter full of memories of our visits. I tell them how important that time was to me, how someday I want to live like they lived in La Veta—away from the city, close to the land, in a good, quiet place where you can grow your own food and raise chickens and be left alone. With the letter I include a stack of photographs I've taken of my friends, a sticker for a band I love, and a clipping from a monthly fiction magazine I'm writing for. Then I take it to Monica to send.

After that it's more event profiles. Headphones back on. Locust CD restarted. The CD has 20 songs, and most are under a minute. It's a wild, frantic swarm of shredding guitars from Gabe Serbian and Bobby Bray over Dave Astor's drums and JP's bass, along with the b-movie sci fi blasts of Joey Karam's synth—each song a brief but deafening explosion, a flare-up that ends as soon as it starts like the oxygen has been sucked out of the room.

Gabe Serbian is the one I watch at shows. His playing is otherworldly, nimble and rhythmic but brutal. If there's anyone in town I'd like most to be it's Gabe. He's godlike, ferocious, glamourous like some kind of outcast metalhead David Bowie.

When the CD ends, I restart it, and this is how I go about my workday.

Other than the stack of record company promos I need to sift through (most still unopened in their manilla bubble mailers), I have six of my favorite CDs on my desk:

1) The latest from the Dismemberment Plan, *Emergency & I*

2) The Black Heart Procession's new album, *2*

3) a burned copy of *Four Cornered Night* by Jets to Brazil

4) Bright Eyes' *Fevers and Mirrors*

5) Pedro the Lion's newest, *Winners Never Quit*

6) and a promo of the new At the Drive-In, *Relationship of Command*

But mostly I play the Locust.

The promos are usually trash from major labels. Those I take down to Music Trader once a week to sell, which is something you're not supposed to do. Every few weeks I'll get a promo CD from a popstar or a shitty massive radio band that's not out for months yet and the store will buy it for 20 or 30 bucks. That's especially frowned upon by the record labels and PR agents, but a) I don't care and b) the extra money is a good side income and pads out my $9-an-hour temping wage. A hundred bucks a week for promos means $400 a month which is a third of the rent on my apartment. The $1,200 rent is tough to meet and my paycheck doesn't come close to covering it when you take into consideration gas, utilities, credit card bills, food, booze, entertainment, and life in general. Selling records helps. Freelance writing gigs help (though most of those don't pay). With another rent increase I'll need to get a second job. Where I'll find the hours to work that job is another story and that story is one of both horror and mystery. It's the sort of mystery I don't know if I can solve. I'm not that kind of detective. Maybe no one is. Maybe that story is just an end without a beginning or a middle—an end, two words, "You lose."

The first event listing I write is a show at the Ché Café. This one's not on Ed's list. I hit the Xtrem icon, click "Add" to create a new profile, and type in the bands: Botch, Volume 11, Time in Malta, Under a Dying Sun, and Good Day Gone Bad. The show is only a few days away on the 8th of October, but I've just found the flyer in the free section at Off the Record. I write a few lines about Botch and reference the *Ché Fest 1999* CD that has a Volume 11 track on it then click the save button.

After that I put in a list of shows from bands I either hate or don't care about.

Weezer, Blink-182, and New Found Glory on New Year's Eve at Cox Arena.

Bon Jovi at the Star 100.7 Jingle Ball, also at Cox.

Next is the "No Strings Attached Tour" for *NSYNC at the Sports Arena. That one's so bad I decide I need to go. After I add it I email the promotor and request press passes. (She writes back immediately and says, "Totes, sweetie!")

Then it's the Offspring, Cypress Hill, and MXPX at a new arena named after weight loss celebrity Jenny Craig in November.

Going down the list I give Bob Dylan's son's band the Wallflowers a decent write-up because I like their country song "Three Marlenas."

Next, Pearl Jam with Supergrass.

Deftones at Coors Amphitheatre.

Both of which I'm ambivalent about and my writing is reflective of that.

Coors is also hosting Everlast and Santana which sounds counterintuitive

On the 10th of October, just a week from now, is Christina Aguilera and Destiny's Child and I make a note in my planner to get free tickets for Cass and Petra.

Tomorrow, Phish is playing Coors which is maybe the worst of all shows. That one I cross off the list but don't actually type in. The Phish show has been on every list Ed's given me since August and every day I leave it out of the listings and every morning it's back again. Ed keeps adding Phish to the list and the thought that Ed might like Phish gives me a weird, cold, dark, sinking feeling like all the blood is being sucked out of me through a tube. I can understand the Grateful Dead but Phish? Of course not all good people have good taste. Last week, very drunk at a house show in Golden Hill, I told Joey Carr and Tyler that "not all people who like Phish are bad, yet *all* bad people like Phish." That's a false equivalence, but sometimes you intentionally say the wrong thing just to get your point across. Sometimes getting your point across is more about stupid, bold, dramatic statements than truth. Often we listen to bravado over logic. You can use this to your advantage (though I'm not sure what that particular advantage is or whether it's worth chasing. My instincts say no.)

Once I've done all the music, film, sports, art gallery openings, and bookstore event profiles I can handle, it's time to find images. Some are sent directly to me from the artists' management or PR. Those are free. Anything else we have to pay for. Xtrem doesn't allow editorial to add images. That's done by the paper's in-house photography guy Stevie. I send Stevie each photo in its own separate email with photo credit and the request to have it added to the corresponding profile. He'll get it turned around by the next day, but if there's a backlog it'll be a few days longer.

A lot of the events don't have press photos. For those I have a contact list of local photographers in a doc titled "Stringer Database." If I can't find a good free image I'll start at the top of the list and work my way down, emailing to ask if they have certain bands or artists or authors depending upon which section I'm doing. If it's a freelance shot Stevie asks accounting to cut a $50 check for the photographer which Monica in reception mails out along with Friday's independent contactor payroll. Sometimes Ed will send me out to get photos with editorial's digital camera that we call "the Mysterious Robot," but I've never been able to make it work. The photos I take are generally so blurry they look smeared with butter. Polaroids and Kodak disposables I can do. Digital cameras not so much.

After I send the photo requests off I go to the supply room to get a notebook. The coil-bound notebooks they give us have "Special Reporter's Notebook!!!" printed across the cover in a curvy, excited, swooping, brown font I love because it seems like something from another age, a relic of journalism-past. The notebooks are narrow (maybe as wide across as a credit card) but they're twice as long as traditional notebooks—about the length of a sheet of printer paper—and the front and back cardboard covers are thick enough that you don't have to use a table. Mostly I write attempts at fiction, letters, to-do lists, notes-to-self, or stories for other publications with the reporter's notebooks and doing that feels nice, like a sweet little harmless revenge on this place.

Unless it's one of my favorite artists, and that's rare, I don't care enough about what I'm covering for the paper to worry how good my writing is. But the feature. The feature Ed assigned has been haunting me all day. I want to do it right. I want Ed to like it and I want everyone in the office to like it, and also everyone in the city and the state and the world. What I want most is for the world to fall in love with me. That's the plan: write the feature, let the love of the world come pouring in like morning sunlight when you pull the curtains aside. Thinking of this, standing in the supply room, I'm swept up in daydreams. The freelance writing jobs that will come from the feature. The book deals that will come from the writing jobs. I'll do interviews about my work and I'll sign books at bookstores and work from home like a proper author should. The daydream carries me along with it and by the time I break free it feels as if it's been hours. On the way out of the supply room I stuff my jean jacket pockets with brown Prismacolor Artgum erasers because I love the smell of them (which is something like modeling clay, beach sand, and rubber cement. It's a comforting smell, a smell of childhood art classes and quiet afternoons). Back at our cubical I begin my feature notes. At the top of the first page I write "Feature!" and add a few more exclamation points for motivation's sake.

Then I sit.

Sit and stare.

Stare at the page.

My mind stupid and blank and my thoughts swirling ungraspable like incense smoke.

Emily and AJ sit on either side of me typing. AJ to my right, leaning close to his screen, mouthing the words as he types them, the monitor's glow shining on his forehead and on the lenses of the glasses he puts on in the middle of the day and is shy about because they age him considerably. Emily to my left types with one hand, the other holding a pale yellow pencil she turns methodically in her fingers, her nails painted cherry red. She looks both serious and careless turning the pencil in her hand and then I'm daydreaming of doing the same thing when I'm interviewed about my work after the feature blows up.

Emily sees me staring and she sets the pencil next to her mouse pad. (When she sets it down I notice it's dented with toothmarks.)

"What?" she says.

I shrug. "Nothing."

"*Why* you staring at me?" she says with comical emphasis on the word "why."

"*Why* would I do that?" I say, using her emphasis against her.

"Today is fucking endless," she says.

AJ takes his headphones off. "What're you faces of fuck talkin' about?"

Just then Jean Lumpkin pops her head around the corner of our cubicle. "Hiiiii kids," she sings, her moony round eyes happy and excited. Jean doesn't come the rest of the way into our area; just stands there holding the side of our cubicle wall like a cartoon character peaking around a corner. Jean Lumpkin is one of the higher-ups we rarely see. Her job has something to do with administration and the word administration is meaningless to me. It's a word like "executive" or "operation," a word that could be anything and because it could be anything that makes it nothing.

Emily and AJ hate Jean Lumpkin and make jokes about her dying in funny, sports-related ways—sports because Jean is a huge Chargers fan and lets everyone know about it any chance she gets. If there's a game that day she's a garish walking billboard for them.

Some of the ways Jean has died include being eaten by a bunch of wild, drunk football players rampaging through a desolate town. Slamdunked into the world's largest basketball hoop by the world's largest Michael Jordan. Tossed at a baseball player who immediately knocks her out of the park and wins the game and makes everyone happy and also rich for some reason.)

As a rule I try to ignore Jean because she's socially oblivious to the point where she doesn't know when people dislike her and that makes me care about her more than I want to. I'd rather hate Jean, but I can't. Regardless, she's aggressively cheerful and when you're hungover or generally not feeling yourself it's exhausting to be around.

"Hi Jean," I say in a preoccupied voice, hoping she'll leave as soon as possible.

Emily gets up and walks away and AJ turns back to his screen.

"Sooo. James. I wanted to talk to you," she says from her spot peaking around our corner.

The fact that she's still holding the pose makes me so anxious I want to vomit or smash my head into something like a spiked wall or a tree that's on fire.

"Okay."

I look down at Emily's bit-up pencil sitting next to her mouse-pad and I imagine driving it into my neck over and over again until I'm dead.

"We're doing a commercial for the site. A *commercial*." She's very excited about the commercial. "We want you to be in it."

"Like on TV?"

"On TV! You want in on this?" The way Jean says "in on this" makes it feel like "COME ON TEAM LET'S FUCKIN' DO THIS SHIT!"

"Oh, I don't—I don't know, Jean. That's not really my—like my thing?"

Now Jean steps around our corner. She's wearing a lavender pantsuit with a big gold brooch on the collar that's either an insect with its wings spread or some sort of complicated jungle plant.

"How much does it pay?" asks AJ, typing, staring at his screen.

"Well, we, uh—well, hahaha, we don't have the budget for that. But hey, it'll be fun!"

"James doesn't like fun," says AJ, deadpanned. "He hates it."

Jean ignores him. "Soooo. This is a *Christmas* spot. We'll have an actor playing Santa and—"

"Wait, a Christmas commercial?" I say.

"James hates Christmas," says AJ, typing. "James is Jewish."

"I'm not," I say. "But a Christmas commercial. I mean, it's not—like, it's not even Halloween yet. Isn't it a little—"

"—early?" asks Jean, excited. "*Yes*. But there's just soooo much lead time with TV ads. We're asking some of the—" she laughs and breaks eye contact, looking up at the ceiling "—smaller guys on staff if they'd like to dress up as Santa's elves for the ad. It'll be fun!" she says for the second time. "The elves will be you, Stevie from photography, and Ricky Vigil from sales."

71

"Dressing up as elves?"

"Elves!" she says, arms spread wide, then shrugging happily like it's the most unexplainably, bafflingly wonderful idea in the world. "It'll be fun!" Jean does a little dance that involves knocking her hips side to side like she's bumping them against an invisible dance partner at a wedding.

"Jean. Uh. No. I can't—"

"*Yeaaah* you can! You'll be *greaaat!*" She flaps her hand dismissively at me. "You'll be a *natural.*" The wedding dance happens again and as I watch Jean dance I understand why Emily and AJ tell stories about her sports death.

"No. No. I, uh, no." It's all I can say. No's. A whole line of them.

"It'll be fun! Thiiink about it!" she sings as she steps back around our cubicle.

AJ turns and stares at me over his glasses. He shakes his head. Doesn't say anything. Just shakes his head.

"Yeah. Fuck this place," I say. "My failure's finally complete. It's time to end it all. Wanna join me?"

"My soul is prepared," he says. "How's yours?" It's a reference to *Indiana Jones and the Last Crusade* and that makes me laugh and when I laugh I stop caring about Jean's shitty elf idea.

Emily sits back down to my left with a cup of coffee.

"What'd I miss?" she asks.

"Our boy here is making his acting debut as a Christmas elf," says AJ. "It'll be *fun*, James."

"James! No!" says Emily. "You *cannot*. Please. Promise me."

"I promise I will never be an elf."

"Thank you."

I put my headphones back on, pick up my notebook again, and underline the word "Feature!!!!!!" and all its exclamations points.

I sit for ages staring at my notebook with absolutely no ideas coming to me. Then I draw a cobweb in the corner because it's almost Halloween then a smiling jack-o'-lantern in the other corner. I draw a happy looking Day of the Dead skull then give it a ribcage chest, skeleton arms, a pelvis connected to a section of spine, and legs ending in cowboy boots. I take my time on the details. Shading. Tiny stitch marks on the skull. A sombrero on its head and a bandoleer of bullets like a soldier in the Mexican Revolution. Then a sword in its hand. Or a saber—yes, a saber, sharp end down like a cane.

A few minutes before five o'clock people begin to pack up. It's the same as at the end of a school day. You hear zippers from backpacks pulling shut, muffled conversation, the clunking sound of a thermos or a metal water bottle hitting something, laughter from down the hall, doors shutting, someone singing indistinct words.

Emily and AJ say goodbye to me then walk out together talking about getting drinks at the Lancers. Ed looks over the top of the cubicle and tells me to have a good night and reminds me that tomorrow we're taking a Tijuana Board of Tourism press junket over the border to Mexico. The news guys file out without saying anything to me. Then it's quiet. Nothing but the on-noise of the computers and the distant sound of the fax machine as it prints a document. I turn the Day of the Dead skeleton page back over the coil and at the top of page #2 I write "feature."

I stay at the office until seven trying to write my feature but all I get are a few more pages with "Feature" written at the top and more drawings—a cartoon dog using a big stick that looks like a tree branch to beat the hell out of a cowering Brendan. A drawing of our office building with a giant dressed as Robin Hood about to step on it and the giant is wearing cool sunglasses and looking straight at you and giving a big cool-guy thumbs-up. (A cartoon speech bubble next to the giant's head reads, "Cool," which makes me laugh as I write it.)

The only time I like being here is when everyone is gone. I don't have a computer at my apartment so this is when I try to write fiction or meet freelance deadlines—the building quiet, the windows dark. Sometimes I think I could write until morning, doesn't matter what, just to feel the keys under the tips of my fingers and watch the words jump to life on the screen and race to the margins, just to *write* because when it's good I feel safe, at home—a world to build and the possibilities endless. But not today. Today I'm a failure and a loser and an idiot kid with no ideas and nothing I do is going to change that. At least not now. Not this week. Not until the weight lets off me.

You can't write stories when the story in your head is one line— *die, die, die.* You can make jokes to lighten the strain and you can laugh but writing? People say you've got to suffer to make art. When I suffer I'm like a walking corpse. If I'm happy, if I'm safe, that's when I can write.

I'm not sure whether the suffering artist thing is a myth or a joke or a scam or some ugly combination of all three. Whatever it is it's a load of poisonous, self-defeating horseshit. We all suffer. Pain is something to heal from not romanticize.

I decide to give up.

At least on today.

On the working part of today.

Sometimes giving up is the final stage of too many blows or the result of a long-building failure.

Sometimes it's you realizing you need a break and giving that as a gift to yourself.

The gift of giving up.

So, here you go, James.

A gift, you lucky dog.

On the way out I steal a few bags of bright green rubberbands from the supply room because they feel nice to squeeze while you drive when your head is full of shitty, awful thoughts. Then, with my shitty, awful thoughts and rubberbands, I take the 163 to the 805 to the 52, and meet Lil' Cassidy at the Ché Café.

The Ché is an all-ages club on the UCSD campus that my friends and I spend a lot of time at. ("Ché" is both a tribute to Guevara and an acronym for "Cheap healthy eats.") The building it's in feels more like a rickety, backwoods cabin than a music venue—a secret, private clubhouse where you have to be a good, decent person but beyond that anything can happen. It's both lawful in a moral sense and lawless.

The wooden shack walls outside are painted with murals of famous activists and radicals; inside there's a magazine rack full of anarchist literature and ratty issues of *Maximum Rocknroll*, a few couches near the stage, a table for merch, a counter window to order vegan food made by college kids, and bathrooms tagged with 20 years of graffiti and band stickers.

The club sits on the edge of a eucalyptus grove with wild rabbits ducking in and out of the underbrush and places to hide in the woods from campus security and drink or have sex or do drugs, and this is where I find Cass, cross-legged on the ground, leaning against the trunk of a fallen tree in the moonlit darkness trying to make a fire. She looks up when she hears my sneakers crunching across the dry leaves and she says, "James Jackson fucking Bozic, how do you start a fire because I cannot for the life of me do this. I would *die* if I got lost in the woods."

I kneel down across from her. "I don't know. I'm terrible at fires."

"C'mon, babygirl, you were a Boy Scout."

"Cub Scout," I say. "Not the same."

"What's the difference?"

"Cubs are little kids."

"Gimme some of that Cubby Cub wisdom."

"Uh, well, I guess first off don't use matches."

"Matches are what I gots, yo."

"It's too windy."

"Bitch, no *doy*."

"Maybe somebody at the show has a lighter."

"James, you know I don't talk to fools I don't already know."

"I'll be your emissary."

"Naw. I'm done. I give up." Cass throws the matchbox off to the side and I crawl over on my hands and knees and pick it up.

"Okay. I'll try."

"Be your best friend if you can start it."

I drag the red top of one of the matchsticks along the gray side of the box.

The match makes a fizzing sound and before I can cup it with my other hand it goes out.

"Fuck. Sorry, Cass. I can't do it either. The wind. Let's go inside. I'll find somebody with a lighter."

Cassidy makes a face like she's smelled something rotten. "I was only there for like a sec and it smelled so much like sweat I had to fuckin' bounce."

"The Ché always smells like sweat."

"Like—like dirty *shirtless* hardcore dude-boy sweat," she says, waving a hand in front of her face. "Pee yew."

"Why do people say 'pee yew' when something stinks?"

"Why?"

"Yeah. What's it stand for? Petunia Unity? Party Urchin? That's a good band name."

"James, stop saying gibberish."

"Pompous Ugly?"

"James. *No. Stop*," she says like she's talking to a bad dog. "Listen, no one knows what pee yew is. It's—James, it's the world's greatest mystery." She stares up at the trees surrounding us in the darkness. "We're on a *campus*. Go ask a *professor*. Go find a professor and be like, 'Hey nerd, I got some questions for you and you better answer them or you're gettin' pantsed.'"

"Do you think anyone's ever pantsed a professor?"

"*I* would," she says. "I *hate* professors."

I laugh. "What? You hate professors? That's a new one."

"Yeah, fuck professors. Go find someone and explain a theory to them. Go eat an apple, you fucking *graduation owl*."

We both laugh and even though it wasn't that funny I can't stop laughing and because I can't stop laughing Cass can't either and we're useless for a few minutes.

"Oh my god, that wasn't even that *good*," says Cass, tears in her eyes, fanning her hands in front of her face like she's trying to cool down. "We need to *stop*. Oh my god."

I try to agree, but I'm laughing too hard and it comes out like, "Ahh new ry?!"

After a while our laughter dies down and Cass curls up on her side next to the fallen tree and I lie back on the soft bed of fragrant, dry leaves.

"This is nice," she says.

"This is very nice."

"James, I'm pretending we're camping."

"That's a good thing to pretend."

"Camping is so much *fun*," says Cassidy in a soft, quiet, fake-excited voice. "I'm glad we're *camping*. Pass me a granola bar. Where'd you put the ranger hat? You bring a canoe?"

"We'll go ride around on the canoe after this."

"Maybe we can see a bear," she says.

"Yeah, totally. A bear grabbing a fish from—like, from a stream or eating a bunch of honey from a pot or having a jamboree or something."

"James, if a fuckin' bear showed up I'd be like, 'Aww, you're so cute. Don't kill me' then I'd fall down and die."

"Don't die, Cass."

"Okay. I won't."

Above us the leaves of the eucalyptus grove rustle in a whispering sigh. A tree trunk creaks when the breeze picks up and the sound is a pleasant thing, like the creak of an old door, the groan of a rocking chair in a cabin.

"Let's go to the show," I say, but Cassidy has fallen asleep. "Cass. *Cass*. Hey. Wake up."

"What? No. Huh?"

"Cass, let's go to the show. I wanna see the Locust."

"I'll stay here. Come back for me." She sits up and says, "Ooh, wow, I slept *hard* for a sec."

Inside the club it's very dark and crowded. The window to the courtyard is foggy from all the bodies in the room and the Locust is on stage, halfway through a minute-long song I love, then half a minute later the song is over. The band is all dyed black hair and denim, dirtbag glamour, sketchy like someone who would steal your car and smash it into a wall just because they think it's funny. The crowd is talking, shouting, the room loud, warm—no, hot, it's hot. There's tension in the place, but it's a good kind of tension like when a fight breaks out and your friends are in it and you have to act. Now. Without thinking. And you act and it feels good. You are swept up in the violence and you know violence is bad because *of course* you know violence is bad, but sometimes violence feels healthy.

There are people in costume in the audience. A boy in nothing but cheetah print bikini briefs and a clear plastic mask with bright red lips. A topless girl wearing a sky blue *luchador* mask and silver tights. There's a lot of hair, thick black dyed hair, Vulcan bangs, sleezy rattails, Joan Jett mullets, eyeliner, tight jeans, colorful new tattoos, kid-size blazer jackets worn in new wave cokehead fashion with a thin necktie, scarves even though it's hot, ridiculous gold mesh or decorative chain-link fashion belts last worn by rich old women in the 1970s, and endless black t-shirts with the sleeves cut off. I look around and see some-one I know then they're gone in the crowd and someone else bumps into me from the back just as the next song starts with a frantic blast of drums. The rest of the band comes in like ro-botic insects attacking you, the music brutal yet contained, heavy and vicious though precise, the song structure like puzzle pieces, interlocked but different, changing in wild, melodic, shredding lines to something else before you get used to what was there first, a ripping surge forward, a sudden stop, a sideways push that could knock over a wall. It's a beautiful thunder, a thunder like new worlds forming. Whenever I see the Locust play I think of a line I love from the Minutemen: "This is Bob Dylan to me." Bob Dylan is also Bob Dylan to me, but the Locust maybe out Bob Dylans him. The Locust is my American folk standard and my campfire protest song, my voice-of-the-people and my this-is-how-it-is.

I watch the rest of their set, then buy a Locust pin, a palm-size makeup mirror with their logo on it, and a puddle-shaped 7" record from the merch table, and cut out before the headliners set up.

Walking back through the woods I see Cass finally got a fire go-ing. It's a brief flash of red in the darkness and it lifts and drops with the breeze, lighting the trunks of the eucalyptus trees all around her with a warm apricot glow.

When I get close I notice she's sitting next to Joey Carr who sees me and waves both arms over his head like he's signaling a plane to land.

At the drugstore we walk down the bright-lit aisles of makeup, the gold tubes of lipstick like shining brass bullets, nail polish in dozens of candy colors, then toys, puzzles, a model Patton tank in a shrink-wrapped box, a rack of Slinkies, discounted *Star Wars* figures from the new movie, bags of Army men, bags of cat's eye marbles, bags of plastic dinosaurs in primary colors, Barbies in tall rectangular boxes, half-price Cabbage Patch Kids, then Halloween decorations and costumes on our way to the wine section.

Joey Carr, who's obsessed with the airline industry right now, walks ahead of us pointing out things and narrating our journey. "On the left side of the cabin you will see a wolfman mask that looks like my uncle's ugliest friend, the legendarily ugly Tony Randazzo. To the right side of the plane please notice the selection of fake spider webs, vampire teeth, witch hats, *Scream* masks, pirate hooks, bloody hatchets—oh, and pitchforks! Pitchforks, if you want to make Jesus mad and go as the Devil this year. Jesus will get *crazy* on your ass. Watch out for crazy Jesus!" Joey idolizes Cassidy and when they hang out he tries desperately to entertain her. This is what he's doing now. "Coming up ahead as we leave the Halloween section you'll see a flock of wild Arizona ice-tea cans, SoBe lizard milk, an elusive herd of Peach Snapple, then soda, juice, Hawaiian Punch, lemonade, and—" and the wine section "—and the wine section!"

Without looking at anything else I grab a jug of Carlo Rossi burgundy because it's all I can afford while Joey and Cassidy debate the selection of cheap reds before choosing beer (and choosing to steal it).

I walk to the register while Joey makes a show of dancing down the makeup aisle wearing a Dracula mask and jabbing at things with a plastic pitchfork so Cassidy can walk out the sliding doors with a case of Tecate.

I pay for the wine at the counter then grab a Bic lighter and a bag of M&Ms at the last minute and pay for that too.

The blonde goth girl behind the counter hands me my receipt and says, "Your friend totally just stole, didn't she?" She stares at me, emotionless, eyes raccooned in black like a chola. Her hair is dyed ice-blond. It's straight, kind of limp, parted down the middle, and she wears a black leather choker around her neck, the ends joined in front with a stainless-steel ring.

"Sorry," I say. "I can't control her. She's a wild animal."

"*I* don't care," she tells me, looking down at the scanner in her hands, turning it in a circle as she talks. "I steal from this place too." She lowers her voice, "You can just take whatever."

"Naw, it's cool. I'm rich."

She laughs and looks up at me, her eyes startlingly blue with the black all around them. "Yeah, me too. But, like—y'know, keep it in mind."

"If I ever lose my fortune," I say, before I realize I'm flirting.

"If you're ever ruined, you come here and I'll hook that shit up. My name's Ruby," she says, tapping a fingertip on her name badge. "You're friends with the Ben Frank kids, aren't you?"

"Yeah. You know them? I'm James, by the way."

"Yeah, I know. I've seen you around," she says, shy, looking down again. "You hang out with Frankie Alicio, right?" I nod, and she says, "I'm friends with her sister Sadie."

"Oh, cool. Sadie's great."

"I know her from *Rocky*," she says, meaning the weekly *Rocky Horror Picture Show* singalong screening they do at La Paloma in North County.

"I've only gone once," I tell her.

"You have fun?"

"I don't really know the lines and all that stuff? But yeah. It was good. It was fun. Sadie played, um, what is it—I can't remember who's who."

"She's usually Columbia."

"See, I don't know anything."

"What're you guys doing tonight?" she tugs her earlobe and I notice her nails are painted in silver glitter.

I jerk my head to the left in the direction of the parking lot. "I'm taking them to Black's so they can do acid."

"Oh shit. Sick."

"You wanna come?" This is something I never do, and as soon as the words leave my mouth I'm sent into a panic. "I mean, like—"

"I wish. My boyfriend's picking me up—" she looks at her watch "—in like 10 minutes. We're going to Sushi Deli. It's our anniversary."

"Oh congrats."

"Thanks."

"Okay, see ya 'round."

"Yeah, see ya," she gives a little wave without raising her arm.

In the empty parking lot Cassidy and Joey sit on the trunk of my car drinking beer. I drop down cross-legged on the asphalt facing them and unscrew the wine cap.

Taking a sip and setting the jug back down, I lie back on the warm pavement and stare up at the sky—black, gray, no stars, just like there are always no stars.

The ground beneath my back is rough and I consider scratching myself against it, but I don't want to look like a bear and in that moment I realize not wanting to look like a bear is silly so I rub my back into the ground and it feels great. "I'm a bear," I tell them as I grind my back to a pulp.

"No more bears," says Cassidy. "This shit's getting too natural for me. First it's bears then it's, like—stupid crap like druids and hippies dancing all over the place and dumb-asses bowing to crystals and everybody wearing big hats."

"Yeah, no big hats, please," I say, working my back into the concrete.

Joey laughs. "James, you look like you're doing some kinda avant-garde dance."

"It's funny because I'm actually not an avant-garde dancer," I say, sitting back up.

"What happened to you in there?" asks Joey, taking a can from the box and snapping the tab open. "Did you die?"

Cassidy says, "We figured you died. We were writing your eulogy."

Joey nods, "Yeah. It was super funny. We rhymed James with flames like you're in hell now."

"I think I asked out that blonde goth girl at the counter."

"You think?" says Jocy.

"Yeah, no, I *know*."

At that moment I see a star.

Then I realize it's moving.

A plane.

"She was cute," says Cassidy.

"Yeah. Yep."

Cass hops off the trunk then leans against it. "You got shot down. Didn't you? I can tell by your mew mew mew sad kitty face." She takes a sip of her beer, happy. "Your ass got *declined* like a fake ID. Let's hit the road, dummies!"

Joey and Cass eat two hits of acid apiece on the drive to Black's Beach. I'm the babysitter tonight. I'm always the babysitter. It's understood that I will drive us home unless we decide to sleep in the car or on the beach and that I will keep the conversation away from dark topics, especially Cassidy's mom and Joey's parents, but also god, illness, old age, death, and war, and make sure no one wanders off and drowns themselves.

We park in the dirt lot and I empty my KPBS tote bag into the trunk and pack it with beers and Cassidy's ancient, faded Strawberry Shortcake beach towel.

As we walk across the deserted parking lot toward the edge of the cliff we talk about our plan of attack. Cass wants to take a path down the cliff that people call "the Ho Chi Minh Trail."

"This shit's basically my birthright," she says. "The only way down this cliff is the Ho Chi Minh unless you're or a fool or a coward. You fucking pacifists can take the Everybody Path. Not me."

Joey is steadfastly against the Ho Chi Minh; tells us he knows someone who fell into the crevice last year and "broke their neck in nineteen-hundred places." He says crevice like "cray-vass" and each time he says it the second vowel is longer and the put-on New England accent more pronounced and he and Cass are laughing more and more which is when I realize their acid is coming on.

They follow me along the half-mile "Everybody Path" also known as "the Goat Trail" that winds in a series of switchbacks down the sandstone cliff to the beach 300 feet below. Cass and Joey are giggly and happy, and they're beginning to make less sense.

"James! Look at the *moon*!" shouts Cass walking in the darkness behind me. "It looks like a big round Joey Carr! Where *is* he?"

"Right here," says Joey, laughing. "He's walking next to you and he's not the moon."

Cass sings a song to the tune of "Riders on the Storm" by the Doors: "Joey is the moon. Blonde goth girl made James swoon. Shitting on the moon."

Joey sings the next verse, "Shitting on the moon. Tender age in bloom. James is seeing spoons. Apes are eating prunes."

Cassidy tells us she'd love to be the first person to take a shit on the moon and that I'm holding the wine jug like a moon, no, like a *pumpkin* in my arms and Joey says, "We're totally calling James 'Linus' from now on. You're okay with that. Right, James?"

I stop mid-trail and sit down and twist the cap off the wine. "Linus is the best Peanut."

"I like the *dirty* one," says Cass.

"Schroeder?" asks Joey.

"I don't know. The dirty one," she says. "Like dust clouds coming off him or whatever. He's fuckin' dope. I would *love* to be that dirty."

Joey and Cass sit down on the hardpacked dirt path. Behind them the trail drops off to a steep, rolling fall, the gray strip of beach far below and beyond that endless black sea and black sky. In the darkness the cliffsides look like something from Greek mythology, the sandstone wrinkled and folded in sections like the skin of an elephant, dotted with darker patches where life clings to the cliffside—ice plant, sage, cactus, dry scrub brush.

Cass sticks two cigarettes in her mouth at once and tries to light a match.

"It's Pigpen," I tell them.

Cass takes the cigarettes out of her mouth. "What is?"

"The dirty Peanut. His name is Pigpen."

"Oh, yeah, the dirty boy," says Cass. "Man, I am fucking *done* with matches."

"Oh! Wait! Get ready for this." I pull the lighter I bought at the drugstore out of my back pocket. "I forgot. Happy birthday."

"Oh shit dude!" says Cass. "You magician. Did you really just do that?"

"I did. I really did that."

"Fuckin' Harry Potter here and his magic tricks," says Cass before lighting the cigarettes and handing both to Joey who laughs and takes a drag off both at the same time then hands one of them back to her.

I stand up. "Hey, alright. Got a long way to go."

Joey laughs, looking up at me. "Did you just do a John Wayne impersonation?"

"Nope. That was a me impersonation."

"It was really good whatever it was," says Joey. "Is it weird that you're called James but there's only one of you?"

"What?"

"Your name is plural. That's weird, right?"

"Yes. It is," I say matter-of-factly before reaching out a hand for Cass to pull her up, then Joey.

Down on the sand, the tall cliff face behind us, it's so dark I can barely see Cass and Joey. The ocean booms, roars. It's loud—loud and vast, black except the lines of whitewash rolling shoreward, long and gray against the field of darkness. The sound of the sea slows my thoughts and I think of childhood pirate stories from picture books then the Berenstain Bears book where the bear family travels to the seashore on vacation and everything goes wrong. I think of fish markets in Point Loma with nautical décor, paintings of Cape Cod lighthouses, and summer days as a kid on my dad's boat staring at the bobbing coastline when I was meant to be fishing.

For a moment—just briefly, as my thoughts cycle and stack up—I think of death, of drowning myself, but that passes quickly, and I'm back on the soft, dry sand walking with my friends, listening to Cass talking about coming here as a kid to look at naked people because Black's is clothing optional; Joey butting in with comments that come out of leftfield, his own teenage beach stories that get stranger as they near the end.

We walk along the waterline until we spot a fire ring someone's made with stones up the beach near the cliff.

"Boom! Fire ring!" says Cass, pointing at it.

"Fire. Oh, fire is safe," says Joey like he's trying to convince himself. "Fire is *not* too hot."

"No, it's like—like, really, *really* hot. But you're okay," I say, resting my hand on his shoulder as we walk. "We're cool. We're fine, Joey. I'm watchin' out for you." His shoulder feels like a skeleton's shoulder, bone, hard, nothing soft, and I pull my hand back.

At the fire ring I take the drugstore receipt the blonde goth girl gave me and the first few pages of drawings from my notebook. I crumple them up together and make a pile of driftwood in a pyramid over them.

Cass says, "Hey. Look at James. He was a Boy Scout."

"Cub," I say as I set more driftwood over the paper.

"I was a Weebalo," says Joey. "Wait? Is that real? Did I just make that up? Weebalo is a thing, right?"

"You go into the Weebalos after you're a Cub," I say.

"What kinda fucking name is *Weebalo*?" asks Cass.

"It's a portmanteau," I say. "Means 'We'll be loyal scouts.' I think it's maybe, uh, like—when you're eight or nine? Joey is that right?"

"I think so," he says. "But I don't know anything right now."

"Weebalo." Cass shakes her head. "That's the stupidest shit I've ever heard."

I flick the lighter on and hold it to the paper and the fire jumps to life, the flames dancing across Cass and Joey's faces. Joey's face—pale, angular, dark circles, a mop of dyed black hair. In the firelight he looks like a vampire cubist painting of himself. Cassidy's face—dark brown normally but honey gold in the light, her eyes deep black and catching the glow, her buzzed head lending her a statuesque presence, like the bust of a pharaoh. Joey looks starved, desiccated, unhealthy, but Cass has the sturdy vigor of an athlete. As frail as she is from all the speed and coke she does, she looks powerful, robust, vital. Joey's like Cassidy's Dorian Gray painting she hides in her attic that decays instead of her. I can't tell whether he'd be horrified to hear that or proud beyond his wildest dreams.

Cass sits cross-legged, back straight.

Joey lies down and tucks his hands under his head.

The sea air is wet, tangy with salt.

I breathe in and it feels healthy.

I say "Sea air" out loud. "Healthy sea air."

For a long time we stare at the fire and say nothing.

"Two and one," Cass says after a while, and I see the light is dancing in her eyes and I can tell she's out of her mind. "Where's the three? The three's like a backwards B with the line cut off. Flip it around. Cut it off. I can't *believe* it."

Joey sits back up, stretching his arms over his head. "She was like, 'Where's the three?' She said, 'Hey guys, where's the three?' Because the three is out *there*," he says, pointing over his shoulder with his thumb. "It's there in the—in the *dark* behind us and we are—*nope*. Yeah. No way—*not* going over there. No. Fucking. Chance."

"Joey, it's okay," I tell him. "That darkness has got nothin' bad in it. I got you guys."

"Isn't there a witch out there?" asks Joey. "Like a witch who lives in a dungeon and spends all her time stirring a big cauldron?"

Cassidy laughs a mean laugh. "Stupid witch."

"Nope," I say. "No witches out there. Nothin' but sand, and sand is your friend."

Cass begins to sing a song in Vietnamese. It's low and soft and pretty. The melody rising like the sparks that float up from the fire.

I take a good, hearty swallow off the jug of Carlo Rossi and listen to her and feel the night breeze on my face and smell the wood burning and all is alright.

"What *was* that?" I ask when she stops.

"What was what?"

"That song, Cass. It was nice. What was it?"

Cassidy looks at Joey like I'm making no sense. "That guy right there isn't a person. He's a bird. Am I right?"

Joey stares at me for a long time, the firelight in his eyes. "Naw, he's not a bird," he says. "They love seeds, don't they?"

"Birds are all insane," says Cassidy. "Don't get near a bird."

Later, as the fire dies down, Joey and Cassidy curl up together on the towel, Cass behind Joey with her arm around his chest, and they sleep.

I get up and walk to the shoreline, squatting down to grab driftwood along the way.

At the water's edge, I stand with the bundle of dry sticks in my arms, the silver-black sky towering above, behind me the cliff face like an angry tidal wave.

The surf is loud. It's a good sound. A sound to fall asleep to.

Back at our camp I drop a few sticks of driftwood on the fire, fold up my jean jacket like a pillow, and lie down with my hands laced behind my head.

The fire comes back to life and crackles merrily and the surf howls crashing and above us the stars are bright and scattered across the black sky as if tossed in handfuls.

Wednesday, October 4th, 2000

I wake up at dawn. Across the fire ring from me, the fire having long gone out, Joey and Cass sleep curled-up together like cats and their empty beer cans dot the sand around them. It's fog-gy—foggy and gray and quiet with a gentle breeze. It feels as if we're an island in the fog or a life raft—the only people for a thousand miles, us here, Joey, Cassidy, James, our spent fire, the beer cans, my wine jug, and all around us a forest of soft, drifting fog as gray as the sand.

You can smell the campfire still. It's sooty, a musky smell, both comforting and exciting.

I build the fire again then take my pen and notebook out of the KPBS tote bag.

At the top of the page I write: "FEATURE" in all caps.

I try to think of the things I love or the things I'm afraid of, memories that have stuck with me, pictures I can't unsee or don't want to forget. I need something tangible, important, something truthful I can write about then tie to the present or connect to the city or an important date in our history (because this is local journalism and you have to keep it relevant to the place). My thoughts cycle through the distant past and through childhood and the present day—*my* present day because if I'm going to do what Ed wants, I'll need to make it personal.

I hunch forward, cross-legged in the sand, the fog surrounding us like a tent, and I write down everything that comes regardless of how journalistically appropriate it is. What I turn in needs to make sense as a feature in a newspaper, but I can figure that out later. I want to get it all down without thinking of what I'm do-ing, to jar myself into remembering, into feeling something. If I can feel it maybe I can make someone else feel it too.

I write my ideas out in a list:

-Fourth grade. Pacific Beach Elementary School. Sitting at my desk in class between Abby Armendariz and Tommi Ramos, staring out the windows which are pure sunlight you can't see out of, white-hot, blinding. The principal opens the door and stops the lesson; her aide Miss Melinda follows, pushing a TV set on a tall metal cart in front of the blackboard, then bending over to plug it in. The Challenger space shuttle has just exploded and we are going to watch the news. Kids all around me start crying before the news even begins and then I'm crying too.

-The grape smell of a scented pen—purple or, no, magenta plastic and you hold the pen to the light and you see the world through it. The loveliness of clear plastic things, colored tint, pink like spring flowers, merry sea blue, tangerine orange. Or clear plastic toys as strange worlds to stare into and get lost in their crystal edges.

-Toys. Peach-colored rubber M.U.S.C.L.E. wrestlers, two inches tall and a vast assortment of characters, more than you could ever hope to buy. A man with a mastodon head. A skinny ninja. A creature in the shape of an oil can with arms and legs. A smiling god with six arms. Later the entire line was reissued in a variety of colors and that was exciting—warm orange that glowed almost neon, a soft and subdued purple, slime green like something toxic. The best were the 20-pack sets you got at Vons or Sav-on that came in an opaque white plastic trash drum the size of a small drinking cup. The fact that there were so many dazzled me. The possibilities felt endless.

-In 5th grade we made cards for the comedian George Burns' 89th birthday because his adopted daughter worked at our school and I pretended to lose mine right before they were due so I wouldn't have to make one. George Burns scared the fuck out of me. He looked like a wise little ape planning something sadistic. If anyone might nuke the world it would be evil George Burns.

-A park at Mission Bay. The cool, chilly sunlight of late-afternoon and the shadows of the trees stretching long across the grass. The smell of grilling hotdogs on the breeze. White paper plates. Styrofoam ice chests. Ruffles in the blue and white bag. Canned sodas. Bright red Coke cans like fire engines. Emerald green 7-Up. The sadness of summer's end.

-The foamy taste of beer the first time I drank.

-The actor Mike Meyers grinning and giving a double thumbs up at the camera.

-*Garfield* comics in the newspaper. Sunday comics in bright, vivid color. *Bloom County. Calvin and Hobbes. The Far Side.* The smell of newsprint—musky, a bit acidic, a basement smell, an attic smell.

-My ex Julia and I burying my family's dog in the backyard and how our other dog sat on the edge of the grave watching her friend get covered up.

-Julia staring out the window as we drove past the bay and how we hadn't spoken all morning and the song on the radio was about seeing stars falling all around someone's face.

-Flags snapping in the breeze at Santa Clara Sailing Center on a rainy fall afternoon, the baywaters gray and ruffled.

-A spring trip to San Francisco with friends a year after high school. Sitting in the back-seat watching the low green crop rows roll by, beyond that the flat blue-white of the sea. Daniel Hannol, driving, tapping the fingers of his right hand on the steering wheel to a jazz song because we thought we were in the Beat Generation that year. In the backseat I'm reading Allen Ginsberg's "Sunflower Sutra" and drinking beer with ice cubes from a Slurpee cup. I read aloud, "I walked on the banks of the tincan banana dock and sat down under the huge shade of a Southern Pacific locomotive to look at the sunset over the box house hills and cry," but they can't hear me in the front-seat.

-In high school when I dropped my copy of *Jane Eyre* in the bathtub so I wouldn't have to read it for English class and it worked because the library was out of copies and I felt like a conquering hero.

-Avocado green cottages in North Park. Honeysuckle. Bees in the rose hedge. Spanish tile courtyards.

-The feeling of an earthworm in your closed hand as a child and how it's stronger than you might imagine.

-Sitting in a dark booth with my grandparents at the Lake Havasu City Pizza Hut. Cheese stretching in strips as I pull a slice away from the rest of the pizza. I smell Italian sausage. The sharp, woody licorice smell of fennel.

-Frankie and I sitting on the sidewalk outside the Empire Club. We're there for the club's all-ages goth night and she's telling me how her dad broke up the family when she was little and sent her and her baby sisters and their mother out west to start their new life. Sent them away. Sent them to California. No, Frankie will write that.

-The sound of the ice cream man driving past and you rush out to meet him before you realize you have no money because you're just a kid. You stand on the sidewalk and watch him drive away and the sky feels vast in a great big blue dome overhead and you're so *small*.

-The sound of a car driving down a wet street in the rain.

-A storm blowing in over the sea.

-A storm blowing in over the sea AND you're home from elementary school, waiting for your mother to bring you a bowl of mac and cheese with cut-up bits of hotdog. You can hear the water boiling in the kitchen and smell the steam and you're very happy but also sad in a way you can't explain. The sky outside the windows—gray, overcast, darkening.

-Looking at toy packages at Mervyn's when I was still too young to read the writing on them and how the letters of the words looked like irregular pieces of metal lined up together.

-A cemetery near the mission up in San Juan Capistrano. The wall around it made of stones set irregularly but a perfect fit. The graves shaded by trees.

-A wedding I went to last week and the reception was at a sad, rundown Irish bar and I played darts and won. At the end of the night the groom cried while singing a song to the bride about how he never wanted to hear her say that she wanted it that way then threw up right there on the karaoke stage.

-The trailerpark we lived in by the freeway and walking down the blacktop street between the trailers toward the pool area's ice cream bar vending machine thinking of creamsicles. Autumn. The smell of maple trees.

-Pine trees.

-Million-dollar gin.

-Bitter grapefruit juice.

-Scrambled eggs with cheese.

-Lewis Carroll.

-Loren Nancarrow.

-Clikatat Ikatowi.

-Richard the Famous Bike Jumper.

-Mercander Carr.

-My uncle Ansel.

-Emerald Street.

-Diamond Street.

-Grass lawns, cut short. The sound of sprinklers tisking.

-The shining chrome bumpers of old cars as you walk past them and for a moment you see some version of your reflection, a carnival mirror image blooming out to a grotesque, swollen parody of you, then gone.

-Spiderwebs.

-Halloween.

No.

None of it.

None of it fits in any sense whatsoever and none of it will lead to a story.

I tear out the pages I've written, ball them up, and stick them in the ashes under a piece of blackened driftwood and they begin to smoke then burn.

Back on campus, in the parking lot behind the Ché, Cassidy gives me a pair of her jeans, socks, and a t-shirt from her car so I have clean clothes for work, and I change in the eucalyptus grove while she and Joey sit on the log from last night and get stoned.

The black jeans are highwaters because Cassidy's short, but I'm not tall either so it's fine. The t-shirt is also black, though faded to smoky gray, with "at.the.drive.in" printed across the front in white and the image of an '80s boombox above it; a shirt of

Cassidy's I've always liked and have twice offered to buy. Over that I throw my denim jacket which now smells like campfire smoke and the day has begun.

At work Emily and AJ are talking happily about what they're calling the "Great American Field Trip." It takes a second after I sit down with my cup of sugar coffee to remember the field trip is the press junket over the border to Tijuana. AJ tells us the van's outside already, and Emily says, "We are going to get so fucking wasted it's not even *funny*." Then Ed's face is above the cubicle wall.

"What's not funny?" he says, smiling, almost laughing but not all the way. "What isn't funny?" He wants in on the joke.

Emily says, "It's nothing" and pulls her red frizzy hair back into a ponytail, puts her headphones on, and AJ gets up and walks over to the table in the middle of the room where we keep a stack of the week's papers from around the world.

"James, what's not funny?" asks Ed.

"Emily was making a joke about us getting drunk down in TJ. It's just a joke, though."

"Wish I was going with you guys."

Ed's so innocently hopeful it hurts my stomach. He's hopeful like a little kid is hopeful—hopeful in a way where you wish more than anything that he'll get what he wants.

"I mostly wanna eat," I tell him. "I'm gonna eat so much I'll die." As soon as the words are out of my mouth I realize it was a weird thing to say and I want desperately to take it back. Ed and I don't have the joking about dying kind of relationship.

"Nobody die, okay? You guys have fun. Maybe your feature can be about that." He dips back behind the cubical wall and AJ sits down with a copy of today's *New York Times*.

"Hey Sweet Baby James," he says. "You wanna hear the news?"

"Sure. Okay," I tell him even though I'd rather not know. This is something I would never admit to anyone, especially here at the paper. I'm happier not knowing what's going on in the world. The bad stories stick with me. As soon as I know about them,

I put the people I love in the places of those who have died, and I can't stop thinking about it until it skips through my head in an awful, lurching, overwhelming loop of the worst images you can imagine—Lil' Cassidy and Joey Carr blown to pieces in the street in Gaza; Frankie and her sisters shot by cops in their mom's house.

AJ reads the headlines aloud to me:

-Arafat Places Conditions on Mideast Talks in Paris

-A Biblical Patriarch's Tomb Becomes a Battleground

-Germany Celebrates a Decade of Unity With "a Bit of Pride"

-The Dearest Eggs Since Faberge, Iranian Caviar Returns

-The 2000 Campaign Transcript, Debate Between Vice President Gore and Governor Bush

-More Shock Waves Over the Mideast

-When the Real Thing Just Isn't Enough

-Yanks Head Home with Series Tied

-A Bear of a Wine Has a Cuddlier Sibling

Emily takes her headphones off and AJ hands her the paper. She turns the pages without looking at anything then sets it on the table next to her. "You guys wanna get baked before we go?"

I don't say anything.

AJ stands up and Emily stands up and they walk away together.

In Tijuana we sit at a café table in a crowded plaza with our rep from the Board of Tourism, Juan Rulfo, a former journalist. Juan Rulfo is also the name of a famous Mexican novelist, but there's no relation he tells us. "I wish," he says, "because Juan Rulfo's *Pedro Páramo* is a book very close to my heart—" he lays a hand on his chest "—but no, it is a coincidence."

Rulfo wears black Ray-Ban sunglasses, gray slacks, and a white oxford shirt with the sleeves rolled up, and his curly black hair is flecked with bits of gray. He reminds me of the actor Benicio del Toro who I like and because of that I instantly like Rulfo. Which is of course a bad reason for liking someone, but the die is cast and I decide we're going to be friends.

Rulfo orders for the table and describes what we're going to get and why it's going to be good and why the plaza we're in is a positive thing for the city and asks us if maybe—he says maybe with a shrug that looks innocent but is most definitely not—if maybe, *maybe* we want beer, maybe some shots. Beer is ordered. Tequila shots are ordered. A margarita is ordered for Brendan who came along to talk about securing ads from Mexican businesses.

Brendan says, "Sooo, are the margaritas the lemony kind?"

Rulfo says, "Lime. They're lime. Here they use fresh limes. They're very good. Don't worry."

We've been at the table ten minutes and Rulfo already hates Brendan. I think he hates AJ too because AJ did a ton of coke on the sly in the back of the van the whole way down, and he's talking a mile a minute to Emily even when someone else is talking at the table.

Rulfo has a very quiet, soft, scratchy, deep voice, and being heard above AJ is hard on a regular day without cocaine, not to mention Brendan busting into the conversation to ask stupid questions I'm sure he knows the answer to.

Some people play dumb just to get in on the conversation no matter what it's about. Brendan doesn't care how he comes across as long as he's heard.

"Margaritas're rum, right?" asks Brendan, his light blue ventriloquist dummy eyes empty and excited at the same time. Brendan's eyes don't look real. Like you could wet your thumb with your tongue and smudge the paint.

The thought of touching Brendan makes my stomach clench tight—a wave of unexpected fear and nausea rolling over me like the moment when food poisoning hits you.

Rulfo ignores him, turning in his seat to face me. "It's James," he says, "James, right?"

I nod and take a sip of my beer then set it in front of me.

"James, after this we are splitting the party up into two of our cars. You and Melissa—"

"Oh. Emily."

He nods. "—and Emily, you two come with me and my driver Hector when he shows up and your friends can take the second car with Tino here," he says motioning toward a tall man in a business suit standing next to the fountain in the courtyard's center. The man, Tino, is talking to a waitress, who laughs, bending forward, arms crossed in front of her, holding a small round serving tray to her chest. Tino the driver pantomimes steering a car, turning an invisible wheel, honking. He pretends to swerve, and the waitress laughs again.

Rulfo gives a little wave and Tino heads toward our table from across the courtyard.

"*Qué onda, chico?*" shouts smiling Tino as he walks, arms spread out like he's welcoming his adoring fans.

Rulfo waves him close, closer, and says something into his ear, hand on his shoulder, then turns back to me. "James, before we jump in the cars, we are going to walk around. I'll show you guys some—some of the *sight*s and then we'll hit the road and head down to the Lopez Winery. It's a bit of a drive, but wait 'til you see this place. You been to a winery before?"

Our waiter sets a shot next to Rulfo's beer and one next to mine.

"*Gracias, compa,*" says Rulfo to the waiter.

"I haven't been to a winery, I don't think. I like wine, though."

He laughs, a little subdued, but it's sincere. "Yes, wine is good. Wine is good. This place, it is like a *fortress*. Not in a bad way. That sounds bad. It feels safe, is what I mean, like you could survive a war in there. One of my favorite places. I'm supposed to say this, you know? It's on the script they give us." He picks up his shotglass, raising it. I take mine and do the same. "I'm supposed to say everything is one of my favorite places, but you know what, fuck it—it's my favorite. *Salud.*"

"*Salud.*"

We drink our shots.

It's good tequila.

Smooth.

A little smoky.

"What kind of tequila is this?"

"Oh, no, no. Tequila I ordered for your friends. This is mezcal. It's like tequila but better. You like scotch?"

"I think I've only had it once. I don't really remember."

"Mezcal is closer to scotch." Rulfo lifts his hand and our waiter standing at a table across the courtyard nods. "James, let's get another round. For us. Your friends can do what they want."

It's a warm, clear, perfect day. Blue skies the color of a nursery and not a breath of wind. The plaza is alive with movement and sound and voices. Small mariachi bands are either setting up in front of storefronts or headed across to the courtyard past the fountain to another gig in their black suits with shining silver piping. Cool teenagers walk past holding skateboards or sodas or shopping bags. Federales with military rifles stand in the shade of the buildings that line the courtyard watching the crowd. It's a Wednesday and that means it's mostly locals, Rulfo tells me. The college kids from the US side start to arrive on Thursday. The tourists, Marines, and Navy guys will begin to show up Friday then invade the place Saturday. Rulfo doesn't say he hates the soldiers and students but you can tell.

"On a day like this, a Wednesday, it is much better to come to Tijuana," he says. "Come on Sunday. Stay for the afternoon. Get a meal. Walk around. You'll have a nice day. Saturday night? No, not so good to be here."

A boy maybe eight or nine in brown slacks and a stained red sweater with a white shirt collar folded over the neck walks up to our table holding a cardboard tray of Canel's gum. The boy smiles (his two front teeth missing) and says, "*Chicle?*"

Rulfo takes a few packs and says, "*Gracias, mijo. Buena suerte.*"

He gives the boy a handful of coins.

Then as the boy walks away Rulfo calls him back and hands him a few peso notes.

When the boy is at the next table Rulfo turns my way. "James, you like *chicle?* Gum?"

"Sure."

I reach out and he sets a plastic-wrapped four-pack of pink candy-coated gum in my hand.

"I always keep some on hand," he says. "My brother and me, we had this thing—this game when we were kids that you kept one of these in your pocket and you would be lucky all day. Mostly it didn't work. My brother, he's a cop now." Rulfo sighs and looks up at a plane passing so far overhead it looks like a piece of cloud. "His life—we live different lives. I don't know if either of us have been lucky. Maybe no one knows when they are experiencing luck. We know when it's bad luck, right? Good luck is just—maybe just you getting through the day. Staying alive, no?" He laughs and nods. "This is the mezcal talking by the way."

"I guess we take it for granted then. Luck, I mean."

"Would you say you are a lucky person, James?"

"No." I pick up my beer then pause before taking a drink. "When I was a kid. Not anymore. Lately my luck is very bad."

"I am the same, I think."

"Maybe today's the day it turns around," I tell him. "This is *also* the mezcal talking."

"You are good to talk to, James. Your friends—eh, not so much. Toast. Toast to talking with new friends and—and to ignoring those who will never be a friend no matter how new they are."

We raise our beers.

The second round of mezcal arrives and Rulfo and I drink a toast to the kids who sell *chicle*.

When Rulfo says the words of the toast I start to tear up and I have to look away and grit my jaw to hold it together.

Emily and AJ are so involved in what they're talking about they don't notice they've been left out of this round.

Brendan has gone across the plaza and now he's kneeling very close to a mariachi band as they play, taking pictures of them with editorial's digital camera.

"You want another shot?" asks Rulfo, pulling a cigarette out of his pack. Rulfo moves like he's very tired or as if something is hurting him, like he's injured his shoulder or has busted ribs. He moves slow, deliberate. "Just one more, no?"

"Cool. Yeah. Just one more. I'm in."

"I figured you would be."

Rulfo lifts his arm and our waiter heads toward us, pulling a notepad and pen out of his apron as he walks.

When our food arrives we stop talking while we're served except for Brendan who is now the only voice at the table.

"Thing I love best about Mexico is it's so *festive*," he says. "It's like every day's a *fiesta*." Brendan says "fiesta" with an unexpected jump in his voice as if he's trying to get us excited.

Emily sneers a little. "Yep. Party, party," she says, twirling a finger in the air.

Rulfo laughs, gets it, knows she's talking shit.

"Festive Tijuanaaaahhh!" shouts Brendan, happily, lifting his margarita glass in the air.

"*A la verga*," says Rulfo under his breath.

I try not to laugh. I know "*a la verga*" from kids back in school. It means something between "What the hell" and "Go fuck yourself."

The large white plates we're given have a variety of food to try. A trio of enchiladas covered in red sauce and melted cheese. A row of small tacos; mine and Emily's with beans, rice, avocado, squash, radish, and cilantro; breaded fish for everyone else. An order of al pastor sopes. A plate of rice with shredded chicken and a plate of tamales in corn husks. On the side there's a red broth shrimp soup, a dish of ceviche, a few baskets of chips, small lava rock bowls of salsa, a blue plastic dish of sour cream, a bowl of halved limes the size of walnuts, and extra tortillas wrapped in yellow paper and aluminum foil, both flour and corn.

As we eat, the tinny sound of forks and knives scraping and clanking against plates, AJ tells Emily, "So I run into him at Rich's again and I'm like, 'Bro. *Bro.* You need to stop coming to my bars or I'll get the wrong idea and think you're just out for my vote.' Flirting. But being *funny* about it, y'know?" Emily nods, taking a bite of enchilada then touching her napkin to her lips before setting it back on the table next to her silverware. AJ continues, "Three drinks later I see him on the dancefloor and he fakes like he doesn't know me. *Ignores* me. I'm like, 'You. Fucking. Cunt.' Can't *believe* that shit. What are we in *high school?*"

"Don't date people in politics," says Emily.

"I know, I know! But he's been out for *ages* so it wouldn't be weird."

"Remember when I dated Jeff Collyer?" says Emily. "He would plan my outfits whenever we went out. It was *exhausting.*"

"I remember that tool," nods AJ.

"He *was* a tool, wasn't he?"

"Black & Decker, baby," says AJ, moving his hand like he's hammering in a nail.

Emily lowers her voice but just barely. "He was also *super* into shaving my stuff. I let him do it once, just once when we were really drunk at his place after a party, and then he wanted to do it all the time. Weirded me out. That's weird, right?"

"I dunno. It's not that weird. Look, Emilyana Zapata, you wanna know my philosophy? I don't have one. Maybe I do—date everybody. You win some, you lose some. If you don't like someone, never call them again. Be cruel. Heartless. Some people are just trash and nothing will ever change that because people don't change."

"You really think so?" she says, shaking salt on what's left of her enchilada. "I think people can change. If people *can't* change? *Ugh.* That's *hopeless*, AJ. That's not a world I want to live in. Even if people can't change I want to *believe* they can."

"They change in small ways and they think that means they're changing but the big stuff? Honey, that shit don't *change*. A piece of garbage will always be a piece of garbage and you need to know when it's time to drop somebody in the dumpster. Look. Here's what you gotta do—"

I excuse myself and walk across the plaza to find a restroom.

Turning right at a shop on the corner selling biker jackets, the smell of new leather sharp in the air, I find myself in a narrow alley with a line of apartments on one side and a tall chain-link fence on the other.

Strung from an apartment window to the top of the fence across the alley is a clothesline, the white pillowcases and light-colored women's t-shirts moving just slightly with a breeze that's just kicked up. When the clouds pass and the sun hits them they're nearly see-through.

To get to the end of the alley I have to walk through the clothes. Ducking under the line, the edge of a damp t-shirt (pink and sunlit) brushing my cheek, I smell laundry soap—floral, industrial—and I imagine hanging myself with the clothesline. Tightening the knot. Twisting in the breeze. Fading from the world. This is something I think of often. Ways I could kill myself. Some of them ugly, others beautiful. A clothesline in an alley? Sad. There's no romance there. Diving into an uneven battle with no chance of return is beautiful. But is that suicide or heroism? Does it matter? I want desperately to live, and also to die.

To live is better, painful but better, beautiful in the way that a warrior is beautiful. Maybe the only beautiful deaths are heroism not suicide, selflessness or altruism rather than self-annihilation. Maybe no death is beautiful at all. Maybe what's beautiful is what we have while we're still here, still seeing the sun through the clouds, still questioning ourselves, still walking through new alleys. With that thought in mind, survival feels like a monument, a fist, a stern set jaw, and then music strikes up in the courtyard behind the wall of apartments—thumping tuba, a roll of snare drum, trumpet, acoustic guitar, accordion, and the singer shouts,

"*Ay yi yiiiiii!*"

"*Ay yi yi*" is something I learned from kids in school just like I learned *a la verga*. It's a way to express sadness, pain, and frustration, but when you say it right it sounds happy.

The music in the courtyard swirls upward like a gust of wind carrying leaves, cascades down, rumbles forward like galloping horses.

Ay yi yi.

I walk to the end of the alley toward the sign reading "*Baños*" painted above a door in white letters on red brick. Next to the bathroom door is another door marked "*Salida.*" I know that word too—exit.

After lunch Rulfo takes us on a walk through the city. We go to the wax museum then a series of buildings with interior courtyards full of shops selling folk art, and after that a record store the size of someone's bedroom.

The bedroom record store smells like the last bit of smoke from an extinguished candle. It's nice. Feels like a place you want to stay all afternoon.

Rulfo and I stand in front of a wall-length rack of cassette tapes.

"What kind of music you like, James?"

"Mostly, like—punk. I guess?"

"I thought so."

"I mean, I listen to folk music and electronic stuff and just plain old, like—like indie-rock or whatever, but we—my friends, we kind of consider all of it punk. It's all—I dunno, like, people who grew up with punk and they might not make music that sounds like it—like punk, I mean—but it's all sort of—sorry, I'm explaining this horribly."

"No, no. Go on."

"It's all part of the same scene but maybe bigger than a scene because it's not like everyone has met each other. But they play the same venues no matter what the music sounds like. Get press in the same magazines. Have the same publicists—and, well, I guess, a lot of the same fans. Know what I mean?"

Rulfo nods and says, "Sure, sure," quietly.

"Like to me and to my friends, this folk band we love called Bright Eyes is punk and this death metal band Cattle Decapitation is punk even though neither sound anything like punk or—yeah, or like each other. Does that make sense? Drinking in the daytime makes me an idiot."

Rulfo says, "My brother, he and I grew up in the TJ punk scene. We were goths and punks at the same time. We had friends who—y'know, they played folk songs or they played ranchero or metal or dance music. It was all one thing because we all came from punk rock. But the—our scene in Tijuana was small. If there was a show? *Everybody* came. Everybody from Mexicali, Tecate, Rosarito, Ensenada. Word got out there's a good show in Tijuana? Mexican punks would hop on the back of a horse to get here. They'd ride a *dog* to get there."

We both laugh.

"My brother—argh, James. He likes *Celine Dion* now."

"That's not very punk rock of him."

"No, not at all punk rock. I go over to his house—my brother, he's got a nice place with a big wall around it up in the hills, much nicer than mine—and he'll say, 'Titi,' that's his nickname he has for me, no one else calls me that. 'Titi, you gotta hear the new Celine Dion song!' and I humor him, I do—you know, because he's my brother and I love him no matter what—then he throws this shit on and sits back on the sofa with his hands behind his head and he says, 'Doaaan get no better'n this, Titi.' What kind of Mexican man likes *Celine Dion*? My brother is who. James, you ever met a cop with good taste in music?" Rulfo pulls a tape from the rack. "Okay. Here we go. *This* is music." He hands me the cassette.

I look at the spine. "They're called Size?"

"*Sí mon,* Size. They were—like kind of new wave? Post-punk? You know what I mean? Kind of goth and punk at the same time just like my brother and me. This one's a live bootleg from—" he turns the tape over in his hands and squints at the writing on the back "—it doesn't say—but early '80s. Best song's called 'Tonight.' Me and my brother, we were *obsessed* with Size when we were in school. We recorded a couple of their shows with our tape player and put out bootlegs on a record label we ran out of our bedroom. Trágico Records—the name of our label. *Very* goth. Very dramatic. We sold them at a stand by Safari's. Got a box of them at home still. Far's I'm concerned they were Mexico's greatest punk band ever. *Buy* that. No, fuck it. I'm buying it for you. Is that a conflict of interest? I haven't been a journalist in a long time."

"I don't care," I say. "I'm not a journalist anyway."

"Why are you here?" he says, squinting at me like I make no sense.

"I don't know."

"I'm buyin' you this tape, James. I don't care either."

We split our group into two identical white Toyota SUVs. AJ and Brendan go off with Tino, the driver who'd been at the plaza, while Emily, Rulfo, and I get into a car with a second driver who doesn't acknowledge our presence. He's an older man, big like a heavyweight boxer, curly black hair receding at the temples and slicked back. He wears the blocky sunglasses that cholos I knew in high school called "Locs" and tan slacks with a white button-up short-sleeve shirt decorated in elaborate, intricate embroidery, and he stares straight ahead as we climb in. Rulfo in the front. Emily and me in the back. Emily to the left like how we sit at work.

"This is—hey, so this is Hector." Rulfo looks back at us between the seats. "He doesn't talk."

Hector starts the car without saying anything and we pull into Tijuana traffic.

"Oh James, hey," says Rulfo, "give me that Size tape."

"Yeah, totally. Hold up." I scratch at the plastic wrap with my thumbnail then tear it off, and hand him the cassette.

"Here we go. Here we go," Rulfo sings, happily as he sticks it in the player then turns it up.

The first song has ominous '80s goth-club keyboards and throbbing bass and a singer who sings in English with an almost British snarl. There's a simple, catchy, ice-cold keyboard solo halfway in and lyrics about butcher knives then another keyboard solo. It's a minute and 17 seconds and it's great.

We drive past dance clubs with open air balconies then cowboy bars with happy people smoking out front and Rulfo looks back at us every few minutes to tell us things about the band. He lists off the band members and tells us how Size almost made it big when they signed to PolyGram in the US only to break up before their debut album was released. He talks about seeing them play a gay bar in Mexico City's Zona Rosa in the early 1980s, and how being gay in Mexico at the time was a dangerous thing. "Still is," he says. "Mexico is not the easiest place to be yourself sometimes. I thought my brother was gay when we were kids and then he gets married to a woman we barely knew. He does that and—it was like he had turned his back on who he truly was. It hurt because it seemed like—ahh, I don't know. Hey—" he points out a synth part and compares it to Devo and explains the meaning behind a chorus. Some of the lyrics are in English, some in Spanish.

I don't realize how drunk I am until we hit the first pothole, the car jolting in a wild, jackhammering stutter like our world is breaking apart. It all comes rushing to me at once—the beer, the tequila, the mezcal. It's like when you're at a bar and you go into the bathroom for the first time all night then you see yourself in the mirror and you realize you're *fucking wasted*. Once that happens you start *feeling* wasted even if you were fine a minute ago and there's no way back from that except to see it through.

Sitting in the car as we rumble over Tijuana backstreets I know this is how today will be and that today will continue to be like this until I sleep or unless something drastic occurs. The thought itself is dark, but it doesn't upset me. I know the place I'm in is unhealthy. It's a place you shouldn't stay long because after a while you become it and it becomes you and then you are indivisibly, inextricably connected to something dark and pernicious. But right now? Right now I don't care about anything because I'm happy in that rare and exhilarating way where what matters is *this very moment*—not what we'll do tomorrow or what we did yesterday or what we might do in some abstract, unknowable future.

As we follow the white SUV down a busy, curving street lined with restaurants and cafes and shops, Emily says, "What do you think AJ's doing right now?"

"Talking," says Rulfo, looking at me in the rearview, and he and I crack up. Emily stares out the window at the storefronts and shops passing—shoe stores, fried chicken diners, seafood restaurants, churches, apartments—and asks if she can smoke and Rulfo says, "No," quietly, as if answering a question from years ago, a question with so much more behind it than a simple request to smoke.

The Lopez Winery sits on a hill overlooking the sea south of Rosarito and north of Ensenada. The desert hills are a deep golden brown and there are no trees—just hard-baked earth, rock, scrub brush, and the fortress overlooking it all. We tour the wine cellars and visit the kitchens and the room where the cigars are made. The walls are stone—thick, modern yet in tribute to something much older.

In a large room with floor-to-ceiling windows facing a view of the silver, wind-chopped sea, we sit on bar stools around small, high, square tables and eat fresh-baked French bread with warm olive oil. The bread is crunchy and dusted with flour on the out-side, hot and soft and fragrant when you break it open. Rulfo brings us wines to taste and tells us about which grape does what and how the olive oil is made here and gives us the history of the area.

After the speech he and I sit with a girl my age who works in the vineyards and we drink a good, dry red wine that tastes like iron and smoke. While we talk we eat more bread with warm olive oil, and the girl picks at a takeaway box of cubed white cheese, green olives, and salami she brought out from the kitchen. Her name is Leti. Rulfo's niece.

Leti's dressed in the blousy, white, button-up shirt, black English riding pants, and stylish knee-length boots everyone at the win-ery wears; her shirt is knotted in front above her belt and her glossy black hair is pulled straight back into a short, thick pony-tail like a matador's (and because of that you can see a circular tattoo behind her left ear of the logo from the punk band Crass.)

Rulfo and Leti talk to each other in Spanish, and I try to follow along, but I'm very drunk now, and they lose me. I can tell they're talking about Rulfo's brother (*hermano*) the cop (*policía*), Leti's dad (*padre*), and that what they're saying isn't good. The brother is doing something neither approves of, something involving money and an art collector or possibly an art gallery in Tijuana, I can't be sure. At one point in the conversation Leti's dark eyes fill suddenly, and she gasps a little and says, "*Aghh*," then laughs as if she's shocked at how fast it (whatever it was—a memory, an idea) came over her.

"*Dios mio*," she says quietly, scrubbing her forehead with the back of her hand.

"*Lo siento, mijita*," says Rulfo, apologizing about something.

Rulfo keeps our glasses full. AJ and Brendan smoke cigars in a far corner of the room and Brendan coughs dramatically every few minutes, fist to his chest while Emily stands at the window across the room from them holding her glass of wine by the stem, watching the sun sink into the west—back straight, one hand on her hip like she's posing for a painting.

I can't be sure but something about the way she's standing, the way she holds her head, tilted a little to the side, tells me she's on the verge of tears. I've seen her like this before. Once at a party late at night in a Downtown high-rise. The memory stops there. That detail alone, and that we were very drunk at the time and she was doing coke and something had gone terribly wrong.

"So, James," says Rulfo. "An online newspaper is not something we had when I was a journalist here. It is one of the first, no?"

"Maybe. I don't know," I say, because I don't. I've never cared enough to find out. "I'm sure there are others. There's no way *we're* the first, but we're—I guess, like, maybe *early*?" The room blurs a little. Rulfo in front of me doubles like some sort of two-headed ogre then pulls back to the center as one Rulfo.

"Sounds like you know your stuff," says Rulfo in a gently sarcastic way. He repeats that to Leti (I think) and she laughs. Her laugh is soft and musical, a good laugh.

"I don't know, man. I shouldn't say this, but—yeah, honestly, I don't give a shit about this job."

"Surely it pays well," he says.

"It would pay well except I'm temping. I make nine bucks an hour. Everyone else makes twice that at the very, like, *lowest*. I mean, I dunno, I just—fuck it, it's okay, I have the least experience of anybody. I don't know what I'm doing most of the time." I'm too drunk to be anything but candid and I watch myself in horror as I veer into self-pity. "I'm the worst writer in the place."

"You're the youngest, though?" he asks.

"Yup."

"You'll be fine. What is, uh—you said *temping?*"

"Oh, like, I'm not officially on staff. I'm temporary, which sounds depressing as shit when you—when you say it like that. I was hired through a temp agency. No benefits, way less money than everyone else. They can fire me anytime without letting me know why. They don't have to give me two weeks. That sort of thing."

"Capitalism," he says with a nod. "Sounds like they're taking advantage of you, my friend."

"Maybe? It's just another—another fucking boring-ass *office* job. Only, people think it's cooler because we're—y'know, quote unquote *writing*. It might as well be a call center." I sip the last of my wine and Rulfo refills my glass. "Thanks. Thank you. But we're not. Writing, I mean. It's not real journalism. What we do—it's something else. I mean, shit, *you know*. You know how journalism is. Some of it's real writing. What the news guys do at the paper is writing. But our shit? Naw, it's somewhere between— between boring, like, *soft,* mainstream entertainment and advertising. What we're doing is fuckin' *worthless.*"

Leti gets up and comes back with a cup of coffee and sets it in front of me.

Rulfo nods at her then says, "I wrote news for nine years and then I was fired for a story, and when I was out—when I was out I was glad to be done. In Mexico we—let's just say you have

111

it easier in the States. You write what you want, say what you want, write about *whom* you want. Here in Mexico? Writing what you want can be bad for your health. Bad for your *life*. A good friend of mine, he was a columnist covering drug trafficking, cartel murders, police corruption. Was on his way to work and a car pulled in front of him blocking the road and some men in another car gunned him down. Shot him to death for what he wrote. After that, and then a few weeks later when I was fired—yeah, no, no thanks," he waves his hands in front of him like he's turning down a drink. "I was happy to be out. I *am* happy to be out. Growing up I wanted to be the *real* Juan Rulfo. I wanted to be Octavio *Paz*. Man, I wanted to be *Borges*, Charles Baudelaire, Fuentes. I was a romantic. I wanted to write like *Joyce*. That's not journalism. What's journalism worth? What's telling the truth worth? A lot. It is. It's worth a lot. But aghh, I don't know—I like my life and I like my family too much to jeopardize that. If I was in the States? *Sure*, yes, I'd still be doing journalism. In a second. No doubt. Maybe at a newspaper like yours. The internet—it's the future, no?"

"Probably. I'm not super into it."

He smiles at me like he's surprised by what I said. "The *future* or the internet?"

"The internet. Maybe the future too?" I laugh, but it's not a happy laugh. "I'm not a big internet guy."

"Nor am I," says Rulfo staring past us at Emily by the wall of windows. "People what, they use it to talk to each other?" He turns to Leti and says something in Spanish, and she replies. He listens for a while and then he says, "Leti, she uses it to talk to her friends."

"I uses, eh—is AIM?" Leti says.

"My friends use that," I tell her. "I guess that's cool if you're into it."

She nods. "Sí. Is cool. My friends says *chilo*. Like same as cool. *Chilo.*"

"*Chilo*," I say, and Leti laughs.

"I guess I understand the internet but—ahh, I don't know," Rulfo says. "There is not a lot there for me. I need to learn to use it better. For my job. For this." He looks around the room. "It will help. I think it will help."

Leti gets up and takes her glass with her, pausing to wrap an arm around her uncle's shoulders then kiss the top of his head which makes Rulfo smile and shut his eyes.

"*Ciao*," she says, softly.

"*Ciao*, baby."

"Is good meaning you. *Meeting* you," she tells me, smiling.

"Yeah, likewise," I say.

When Leti's gone, Rulfo says, "My brother—listen, my brother he had some troubles when Leti was a baby. So my wife and I raised her, Leti, for a lot of years. She's my daughter as much as she is my brother's daughter. I would kill or die for only two people," he holds up two fingers like a peace sign. "For my wife Alicia and for Leti."

"Not your brother?" When I say this, I have a sudden rush of panic that I've stepped out of line, that I have drunkenly, foolishly crossed a boundary I shouldn't have.

Rulfo sighs and rubs his jaw, his eyes tired and lit hazel, the light of the sunset in them. "My brother—yes, I would die for him."

I notice he doesn't say that he would also kill for him, and I don't push it.

On the drive back to the border I'm beginning to sober up, but the edges are still gauzy, indistinct—blurring with the headlights of oncoming cars. Rulfo and Emily are talking loudly about Arnold Schwarzenegger over the pulsing, abrasive dance music coming from the speakers. It's dark now and we're just outside the city limits of Tijuana, the empty desert highway lit with a harsh, sickly yellow light.

"I just think he's for boys," says Emily. "He's like a toy. Like an action figure."

Rulfo, looking at her between the seats, says, "But, argh, *Commando!* Listen, *chingón,* Arnold in *Commando*—one of the greatest films of all time. It's *art.*"

"*Commando* is a boy movie full of boys killing each other. There's nothing there for me. It's like watching football. American football. Why should I care?"

"What do you like?" he asks.

"With film?"

"With film."

"I like Cassavetes."

"Ahh," says Rulfo, "I like his movies too but Arnold—no question. Arnold, he's my guy. Cassavetes makes you think—" he taps his temple with his forefinger "—but Arnold makes you laugh."

"Cassavetes can be funny. Gena Rowlands in *A Woman Under the Influence*? It's dark, it's sad, but she's very funny."

"Ah, *mija,* but different. Sometimes—sometimes I'm too tired for that kind of funny. Life has too much of that kind of funny."

Emily and Rulfo are passing a bottle of wine back and forth between the seats. Hector the driver stares straight ahead—grim, hard like stone, the yellow streetlight tiger-striping his pockmarked face then falling to shadow again.

Rulfo holds the bottle in my direction and I take it after waving off the first few turns. "Yeah. Thanks." I sip it, then I drink more, and when I do that I'm not sobering up any longer. I take another drink and pass it to Emily, who has lit a cigarette and is rolling her window down. "Kill it," I tell her, nodding at the bottle.

Just then the windshield is speckled with rain.

"Raining," says Rulfo. "Hector. *Lloviendo.*"

Hector turns the wipers on, and they clunk back and forth.

"*All* those action movies," Emily says, rolling her window back up with one hand and holding the bottle by the neck and her cig-

114

arette in the other, "Steven Segal, Chuck Norris, Van Damme, fuckin' *Stallone*—"

"Oh," says Rulfo, looking ahead now. "Traffic. I need to—" Rulfo stops midsentence then all you hear is the loud, distorted house music over the car stereo and the rhythmic knock of the wipers. "Shit," he says and you can tell he's serious now.

"What?" says Emily. "What's shit?" She hands the bottle back to me and I finish the last bit.

"James. Stick—hey, stick that bottle under the seat," Rulfo says. "*Quick.*"

As we slow in traffic I see the bodies on the side of the highway.

"Are those—" Emily starts to say.

"Yes, *mija*," says Rulfo. "They are."

To the right of us is a panel van on its side.

Next to the van, in the ditch, are three dead men.

The men are dressed alike in some sort of gray or maybe blue coverall uniform—under the yellow streetlights and this late at night there are no colors except shades of black, yellow, and gray, and red flash of brakelights.

Traffic is stopped now.

Without saying anything or looking at the radio Rulfo turns the dance music station to smooth jazz. It's a lone saxophone playing gently like a flag rippling in the breeze.

Rulfo makes the sign of the cross and stares straight ahead, tapping the fingers of his right hand on the frame of the passenger window as an older woman steps out from behind the van and begins to cover the dead men in blankets from a stack she has draped over her arm. We watch her cover their bodies and when she's done, she stands looking down at them for a very long time, motionless, the brake-lights of cars lighting the wet asphalt red around her, flashing off and on as we inch forward.

Back at the office, AJ and Emily, who are both very drunk, stand next to AJ's car in the streetlight-lit parking lot smoking while I walk to the building to grab my bag. I look back and they're standing close to each other now. Emily takes a drag off her cigarette and rests her head on AJ's shoulder and AJ wraps an arm around her.

At my desk, the office empty and silent, I realize I have the idea for my feature. It comes to me with a beginning, middle, and end, and I know just how to say what I need to say.

Excited to sit down and work, I power my computer up and wait for it to come to life.

The windows across the room from me are black as if they're painted that way, like even if you were standing in front of them, your nose just inches from the glass, you wouldn't see anything outside.

When the story is done I read through it twice then email it to Ed.

It's 2am, but Ed the night owl writes back immediately.

"Hi! We have some people over for drinks, but I've got a minute so I'll read it right now. Brendan's telling us all about Mexico. Sounds fun!"

I put my head on my desk and let my thoughts slow.

I imagine a blank white brick wall in front of me, a wall with no detail, the bricks newly painted, a wall with nothing hung on it, no art, no photos, the paint perfectly smooth, fresh, so fresh you can smell it, the smell of new house paint, new carpet, a new home, a blank slate, a resurrection—I slip off and in the briefest moment I'm running through dark woods with a butter yellow moon above the trees then my leg jerks as the dream-me jumps over a fallen log and my knee hits the underside of my desk and I'm awake.

Sitting back up I stretch my arms over my head then move my mouse and the computer screen jumps to life.

The clock on the computer says I've slept 15 minutes.

When I check my email Ed has written back.

"James, buddy, I appreciate the effort, but this is not a good fit for the paper. Sorry, man. Let's talk about a few things tomorrow, okay?"

I read the message three times then hit delete because deleting feels like undoing it.

Which of course doesn't work.

"Not a good fit" sticks with me. I go to the breakroom and make coffee and get a bag of M&Ms from the machine. "Fuck Ed," I say aloud and to no one and feel stupid for doing it. "Piece of shit," I mumble to myself as I walk back down the hall, but as soon as it's out of my mouth I know the piece of shit isn't Ed.

Back at my desk, the coffee cooling in front of me, "Not a good fit" keeps replaying. It replays until I put my head down on my desk and sleep.

I sleep hard then awake as if trapped under layers of ice and sit up to see the sun streaming in through the windows in the far corner of the office.

Thursday, October, 5th, 2000

At 7:30 I take the elevator down to the lobby and walk out into the morning air. The traffic is loud on Friar's Road, and the wind is up, not warm or cold, just hard, a grating city wind that doesn't care about you. I'm hungover in a way that feels like a fist is opening and closing in the pit of my stomach, hungover like the most fundamental parts of me are all strained and malfunctioning and won't be right again.

Standing next to my car, holding the side mirror for support, I vomit pure, dark, hot red wine onto the asphalt for a very long time then walk around the industrial lot and the empty mall until nine.

When I get back to the office I find Emily typing in front of her computer. She looks up at me as I sit down and says, "Oh man, I feel baaad. *How* many bottles of Lopez wine did we drink?"

AJ isn't in yet.

"Too many I think."

"Yeah," she says. "Too many sounds about right. I too manied my fucking brains out."

I drape my jean jacket on the back of my rolling chair and go to the breakroom for coffee.

Passing by Ed's office, I see the lights are off, the door slightly ajar. His desk is covered in stacks of paper and a pile of manilla file folders. The computer screen is on and the wall behind it is lit as if from a spotlight.

Walking down the hall I hear laughter and shouting from sales then the bell dings.

They've got a sale.

Someone shouts, "We got a sale!" and the bell dings again.

As I walk I wonder if two dings means two sales then I remember that I don't care and that I hate them and hate their bell and hate ads.

No, it's not the salespeople. They're okay. It's Brendan and Do-nut I hate. Donut and his slow motion running and bodybuilder posing and high-fives. Brendan and his shrill voice and his wooden dummy face, Brendan hopping around like a goddamn puppet.

I imagine swinging the sales bell with all my might and slamming it into Brendan's chest and how the impact sends him flying backwards toward the window which he busts through then flies out into the blue sky until he's a tiny speck which then disappears forever. The End.

It makes me smile and then I'm laughing—laughing out loud and my nerves are shot to hell and my hangover boils me like I'm a dry brick of ramen noodles that has been dropped in a pot of water on the stove.

I make a right into the breakroom just as Donut walks out and we nearly bump chests.

"Bro," he says, "I brought donuts."

"Finally," I say as sincere as I can—sincere because a donut sounds good, and of course because Donut himself shouts "*Who* brought donuts?" each morning in the hopes that someone has, and now, finally, he's done it himself. He's taken the reins and brought donuts because no one ever does and what he wants most in life is a fucking sweet, delicious donut.

I tried to say "Finally" in a nice way, but it came out sarcastic.

He turns and walks backward a second down the hall, staring at me like he's trying to figure me out.

Right before he turns back around, he says, quietly, hurt, "You don't need to be a dick, man."

Just then I remember his name.

It's Anthony.

Donut's real name is Anthony.

That's what his parents named him before he'd ever heard of a donut or selling things or bells, before he learned about slow motion or bodybuilders, when he was new, sightless, born or maybe not yet born—yes, when he was a *thought,* a thought to rest all your hopes on, a thought someone loved more than anything.

Anthony.

A baby.

Baby Anthony.

As I walk into the breakroom the idea drives tears into my eyes, fills them suddenly, and I fight to push it away, shove it back somewhere it can't reach me. I *hate* Donut. I shouldn't be thinking of him in any sort of sympathetic way. But I am. I am and I can't stop.

In the breakroom a white box of donuts sits on the table, its lid with the plastic view window open. Pink shiny ones, chocolate, maple, old-fashioned, something frosted white with sprinkles, then others—weird ones, experimental ones. Some of the donuts look like they're from space. Some of them look like science projects or ancient artifacts.

The coffee's still brewing so I sit at the table and eat a pink donut in three bites.

It tastes like nothing.

Like sugar and air.

Just then I realize how hungry I am.

I pick up an old-fashioned, smell it, then take a bite. Another bite. Air and sugar and maybe cinnamon. Better. Maybe even good. I can't tell.

Amir walks into the room as I'm starting on a strange black glazed donut with multiple red dots of icing arranged across the top like the eyes of an evil spider.

"James, my friend. Please don't eat that. It will kill you."

"What's up, Amir. I don't even know why I'm eating these."

"Because you are wanting to die, my friend. Because you hate yourself."

I laugh. "You are not wrong."

He sits across from me and pulls the donut box over to look in it.

"No. This is bad, bad," he says, pushing it back to the middle of the table. "If you want to die just let me know and I will kill you, my friend. Do not go out like this."

"Will you hit me with the sales bell and send me flying out the window, never to return?"

Amir laughs, low but satisfied, and nods his head slowly. "Yes, I would love to kill you in that way. It is an amazing way to die."

"You waiting for the coffee?"

"I am killing time, my friend. Until the big meeting."

"The big meeting?"

"Something big. What I don't know. Attendance, it is mandatory. Is, uh—" he tugs his sleeve up and looks at his watch "—10 minutes until."

"Fuck that shit."

Amir smiles his lovely smile. "Yes. Fuck that shit. I will be there. So will you."

"Did I tell you Jean wants me to be in a commercial dressed up as an elf?"

"Like a warrior?"

"Like Christmas."

Amir laughs. "No, please, my friend. Do not do that. You will regret."

"I like you, Amir."

"I like you too, my friend."

When it's time for the big meeting I take the elevator to the ground floor and walk across the endless mall parking lot to the new IKEA where I get a slice of cheese pizza and a fountain Coke from the bistro downstairs to fight my hangover.

I squat up against the white stucco wall outside IKEA and eat the pizza and drink the Coke and watch the cars pull in and out of the parking lot.

In the clear light of day, and in the morning sun (the wind having quit), I see how filthy I am. My black jeans (Cassidy's jeans) are speckled with food and wine stains, my sneakers have sand crusted into all the folds and gaps, and my Cassidy shirt has grease spots down the front from yesterday's tacos and the olive oil that went with the Lopez Winery bread.

Tijuana was yesterday. It feels like years ago. Sleeping on the beach at Black's and the Ché show were a day before that, housesitting and the rave the day before Black's, but they feel like another lifetime, maybe a movie I watched, or a dream, or something from a book I read and recall only in pieces. Four days. Four hundred thousand years.

The greasy pizza and the Coke work together like heroes to wipe out the bad hangover thoughts, and as I walk back to the office, the paranoia, ache, and nausea lift and so do my spirits and I feel 50 pounds lighter, 100 pounds, all my pounds like I'm floating weightless across the surface of the moon, my feet hardly touching the ground as I leap between craters.

All is wonderful until it's not when I remember the feature. The "Not a good fit" and the "Let's talk about a few things tomorrow, okay?" Those words swirl around my face as the hangover drifts back into me like a dirty, shitty ghost and the IKEA pizza and fountain Coke boil in my stomach and I know it's just new vomit waiting to come up.

Back at the office Ed's still not in. Emily and AJ are in front of their computers, headphones on.

As I sit down Emily takes her headphones off and says, without looking at me, "Where were you?"

Her voice is quiet, younger.

"IKEA," I say.

She turns and looks at me like I'm insane. "IKEA?"

"I bought some bookcases and a bunch of, like, tables and stuff and a couple beds." I say this as a joke.

Before she can reply, and because all I've got is a single stupid joke, I put on my headphones and cue up the Locust and blast it until my brain feels like bread dough squeezed, kneaded, brought together as a ball, stretched apart again, then held safe by the onslaught of violent sound.

I open Xtrem and type in a page of bar and DJ events I didn't get to yesterday. Then art galleries. Music, no. I can't bring myself to do that. I make a Halloween resolution to never write about music again then that resolution becomes never write about art galleries or bars or DJs which turns into never use Xtrem again which is then quit tomorrow which becomes walk out of here at the end of today and don't ever come back, which becomes disappear off the face of the Earth, never see another human being again, especially those I love, cancel my phone line and email, then vanish which becomes die, die, *die*.

That cycle of thought turns and gnashes itself, spins tumbling like a clothes dryer, then I realize I've done nothing but think those awful, worthless thoughts for an hour. Emily and AJ are gone. I take my headphones off, and the place is quiet.

The clock on my monitor says 1:01pm.

I click the screen off, get up, and walk down the hall.

No news guys.

No Ed.

Monica's desk in reception is empty and her computer screen is black.

Sales has cleared out.

I think for a moment of flipping the bell over and pissing into it, but then I remember the security cameras, and how this summer they caught our creepy intern Louie Greel licking the seat of Emily's chair after everyone left.

I go to the breakroom and the donuts are as I've left them. Three gone, mine. The rest untouched. The coffee pot still full.

I pour a cup and the amount of sugar Amir says will kill me then stand and stare at the snack machine selection.

I drink half my cup of coffee while standing in front of the machine then pour the rest in the sink, rinse the cup, and set it upside down on the drying rack.

I walk back down the hall which feels like it never ends because the silence—the *silence* is so heavy it's its own sound, like the small roaring ocean you hear inside a seashell.

Walking past the open door to Ed's office I find Brendan in there thumbing through folders in a file cabinet.

"Brendan?"

He whirls around. "Whoa! Oh my god James you scared me to *death*," he says, hand to his chest.

"Brendan, where is everybody?"

He looks at me like I'm speaking a different language. "You weren't at the meeting?"

"I was at IKEA." Brendan's ventriloquist dummy face stares at me, blank eyed. "Why, what happened? Brendan, they shutting us down?" At that thought a surge of joy rolls over me. Quitting without having to quit. Beautiful.

"James, Ed died."

"Wait. What?" I don't know if I say those words out loud or if they're in my head, so I say them again and maybe a third time as I back up looking for a chair to sit down in but only find the glass wall that divides Ed's office from the hallway.

"My uncle—he—uh, Ed had a heart attack last night. Well, early this morning, I guess. Like 3am?"

"What happened?"

"He had a heart attack."

"I mean, what *happened*?"

"That's all we know. We called a staff vacation for the rest of the day."

"Vacation." I try to say it like a question, but it comes out flat.

"Everyone's gone home. You should too, James."

"But Brendan—"

"I'm taking his position for the time being. Gettin' stuff in order."

"In order?"

"Gonna pull a late one tonight. Big move for me. Sales to editorial!" He says the last three words happily.

"You're—wait, Brendan, you're the *editor* now?"

"For now."

"You can't just—"

"James, we're not sure what's next, but we're trying to—uh, show must go on, right? *Speaking of.* I was going over the storyboards Ed put up Tuesday and I saw he's got *you* listed for a feature. We don't have anything else to run front-of-site tomorrow since—all this," he shrugs comically and as he does that I realize Brendan is a shrugger, he shrugs, he shrugs constantly. "So I wanna put it on the main page. Over at Print they're talking about using some of the online content in Sunday's edition as a tribute to Ed's career and I said they could use your feature and they were up for it, especially when I told them you're our resident kid. Sooo. Like. Good? Yeah?"

I lean against the glass wall because I know if I don't I'll need to sit. "My feature."

"You ready to roll with that? You ready to rock 'n' roll?" He says the words "rock 'n' roll" with a lot of pizzaz, a lot of what feels like jazz hands waving joyfully or rampant school spirit.

"My feature. Uh, no. I'm not. I just—"

"Did you write it?"

"No."

"Are you going to becaaause—" he shrugs again dramatically, eyebrows raised.

"No." I turn and walk out of Ed's office.

"James—hey, James, where—"

I walk back down the hall as Brendan's voice trails off and from the hall to the elevator and from the elevator to the ground floor and from the ground floor to the parking lot and from the parking lot driving through more parking lots then Friar's Road, the 8-West, the exit to my apartment, my apartment's parking lot, the concrete steps up to the sidewalk that runs along the front of the complex, my front door, the dark living room which is also the kitchen (divided by an island counter) and down on the couch next to the answering machine on which I press play and—

"Message One. On October 5th, 2000. At 1:15pm," says my answering machine's computer woman voice.

"*Hey James*, this is Frankie. Tyler and my cousin Alison and I were thinking of going to see *The Source* at the Ken and sneaking some beers in. It's that Beat Generation movie? It's new or something, I guess. Call me."

"Message Two. On October 5th, 2000. At 1:30pm."

"James! It's Cass! Ho! Ho! Ho! Merry Christmas in October you fucking mint chocolatey Christmas elf because Petra just won the *California fucking Lottery*! It's only $1,000 but still. *Still!* We're going down to TJ. There's some pill that's like GHB that Petra read about online you can get in the pharmacies without a prescription and we're getting some and we're gonna sell that shit and make *bank*. TJ. Now. You're comin' with. Call me."

I stare at the wall and think nothing.

Absolutely nothing.

When I come back into my head I realize my apartment smells bad. Like damp carpet. Incense that's musky in a urine way. Spilled red wine. But mostly damp carpet. Maybe it always smells this way and I've been away long enough I'm finally noticing it.

As if stepping away from my body I see myself dressed as a

Christmas elf on a TV screen and I turn to the camera and say, "My apartment smells bad" and behind me on the big throne Santa Claus roars, "HO! HO! HO!"

Picking up the phone from its catch, I punch in *69 and it dials Cassidy's number. I tell her Ed died and to come over then I stare at the wall for an indeterminable amount of time before I snap back to reality and call Frankie's house.

"Hello?" It's Frankie's mom.

"Hi. Is—uh, is, uh, like, is Frankie there?"

She calls away from the phone, "Frances! Hey! You've got a call! She's coming."

The line is quiet for a while. I hear the sound of a dog barking in the background, distant. It's a comforting sound. A regular neighborhood sound. A place where people have houses and they sleep at their houses in real beds not in office chairs or on the beach or in strange, tacky mansions.

"Hello?" It's Frankie.

"Hey." For a second I forget my name. "It's—uh, I'm, um, it's *James*. I got your message a sec ago. Yeah, so, I'm down for the movie."

"Okay, it's at 11. What are you doing right now? You at work?"

"I'm home doing nothing. Sitting around."

"You wanna go get dinner then we pick up Alison and Tyler and head out?"

"Okay. Yeah. Let's do that. Where?"

"Old Spaghetti Factory? James and Frankie Pasta Fest 2000?"

"Pasta Fest sounds great." It does. It sounds extremely fucking great. Warm, soft bread. Steaming marinara. Parmesan cheese. Wine. Mozzarella. Ravioli. Browned butter mizithra. Alfredo sauce. I'm feeling better now and feeling better shocks me.

"Okay, it's a date," she says.

"It is." Is it?

"I mean, like, y'know."

"Yeah." I don't know.

"Pick me up at, like—uh, 8?"

"Eight. Totally, yeah. See you then."

"Okay. Cool. Bye."

"Bye."

Just then a knock at the door.

Cassidy's signature knock—the first five beats of "Shave and a Haircut" without the final knocks of "Two bits."

It's also my signature knock so maybe that means it's neither of ours.

I get up and answer the door.

Cassidy kneels hunched forward on the carpet in front of me rolling a joint. She's careful about it, moving her fingers with the grace of a sculptor, the Ziplock bag of pale green weed next to her knee, the stems picked out and tossed aside. Cassidy's decided to quit hard drugs. Tells me she looked in the mirror last night and saw her dead mother's face and it freaked her out. She's decided to become "a massive fucking stoner and a hopeless, pathetic wino and that's it."

I was made in charge of DJing. After I played the A and B-sides of a Minmae single, I gave up, put on *An Orchestrated Rise to Fall* by the Album Leaf—volume low, enough to hear the drowsy, muffled drag of the needle—and now I'm sitting cross-legged on the couch drinking pretty okay wine from a bottle of Two Buck Chuck that Cassidy bought me with two bucks of Petra's lottery score.

"So, he's just, like, *dead* and no one knows what's up?" she says.

"Just that it was a heart attack. Brendan was over there last night, but I didn't think to ask if he was, like, *there* there."

"Oh."

"Like *there* when it happened. I feel like he would've said."

"Wow. Fuck."

"Yeah. I can't even think about it."

"You quitting?"

"Now that Ed's—"

"Yeah," she says.

"I should."

"How's that lottery wine?" she asks, nodding at the bottle in my hands.

"Pretty okay."

"Thank you, the state of California," says Cassidy.

I take a sip and wipe my mouth. "Thanks, California."

Cass licks the paper and rolls the joint shut.

"You got that sweet-ass Black's Beach lighter?" she asks.

I get up off the couch and go around the kitchen island counter and grab it from the junk drawer next to the sink where I'd dumped my keys and wallet when I got home.

"Think fast."

I toss the lighter over the counter to her.

Cassidy makes her hands into a bowl, catching it with a little wince like it's going to hurt her.

"You're a hero," she says.

Cass lights the joint and takes a drag, blowing the smoke out, one eye shut.

"Last thing in the world I am's a hero," I say.

"I think you're pretty great," she tells me, letting the words hang in the smoky air before she says, "I mean, for someone who's stupid and ugly and bound to fail at everything and die alone." The smoke from her joint trails up around her neck and face, silver in the dusty light from the window. She breaks into a grin and says, "You shitty fucking loser."

I stare at her for a second wondering what to say then I laugh and Cassidy laughs and for a while we can't stop.

After Cass leaves I get in the shower and turn the tap as hot as I can take. I shut my eyes let the water hit the back of my head. I have zero thoughts during this time. My mind drifts off and once it's away I know only the water and the heat and the steam and the sound of the shower.

Then I come back to myself.

I open my eyes and begin to wash.

The water runs off me with black grits of soot and flecks of dirt and sand then I'm singing a Richard Hell song with made-up lyrics about dogs eating their own shit as I dig my nails into my scalp working the shampoo in. My fingernails are sharp, like shards of glass. They hurt me and it's a good pain, a pain like release, like a pressure valve twisted open.

When the water runs clear down the drain I turn off the tap, pull the plastic curtain to the side, and step out onto the soft bathroom rug.

I grab a towel from the rack and dry off. Scrub my head hard, scrub all the shit out, scrub out today, the news of Ed's death, Brendan's takeover, the dead men on the side of the road, scrub away wanting to die, scrub out drinking too much, a week of sleeplessness, me as a Christmas elf, the internet newspaper it-self, scrub it to pieces, scrub it raw, out of existence, out of my memory, out of reality.

When my hair is dry I wrap the towel around my waist even though no one's here to see me and walk down the short hallway to the bedroom.

Standing at the window next to the desk I've had since elementary school and never use, I grab the cord and pull shut the beige plastic blinds, closing off the view into the canyon behind the apartment complex with its dry brush and eucalyptus and palm trees and the row of houses on the other side.

Drop the towel on the floor.

Kick it toward the door before I realize I'm not sure why.

Then clothes.

Plaid boxers from the pile of clean laundry on my thrift shop easy chair next to the desk. Faded, silk-thin, black t-shirt with the words "The Gravetones" in blocky screen-printed white. Black jeans that are usually too tight but are not now. Socks. I find only white ones then dig deeper for a colored pair. A thin red one with purple stars and a faded camouflage one. Fine. Shoes— shoes are under the bed. White pair of Converse All-Stars I've never worn because they're the same as Cassidy's, but a new pair of shoes sounds nice after being dirty for so long.

Shoes pulled on.

Laced up tight.

Nice.

Yes.

That feels nice.

The smell of new shoe rubber.

Nice.

Back in the bathroom I wipe the fog from the mirror with my hand, and take the blue plastic tub of Bed Head from the counter next to the sink. I rub the Bed Head in my fingers until it's warm then work it into my hair and try to make it look cool. I rough up the back so it spikes out a little and pull my bangs to the side. It looks so stupid it makes me want to smash my head into the mirror. I flat down the back again and arrange my bangs how they always look, like Spock, like a Vulcan.

Wanting to smash my head into the mirror makes me feel better. I imagine jerking my neck back then headbutting forward and hitting the glass and the glass fracturing out in all directions, bright red blood trickling in a thin stream down from my hairline as I stare at a cracked version of myself. Thinking about it feels good in a way that makes no sense. Like how violent music feels comforting. How ugly thoughts can be beautiful. How certain kinds of pain can be pleasure. You don't always have to make sense or be positive to feel good. Some of the best things exist outside of black and white truths. They are creatures of ambiguity, chaos, discordance. Living in that particular space can feel like a ray of soft, warm sunlight after a long night. It can feel like an unsolicited compliment from someone you least expect to care. Like a gift, a stay of execution.

To kill time before meeting Frankie I head out to my favorite spot in Point Loma where the cliffs stand high above the sea, the road wrapping along the cliffside. I drive past people gathered near the edge in small groups waiting for the sun to go down, past solitary joggers, dog walkers, surfers in black wetsuits carrying white surfboards, children running too close to the cliff, couples I imagine are out on dates, holding hands or standing together with an arm around a waist or locked in an embrace like slow dancing without moving. Dancing. Everyone together feels like a dance. Sometimes it's a sad dance, but it's still a dance.

I parallel park between a light blue Volkswagen van with Grateful Dead stickers on the back and a motorcycle propped up by its kickstand.

The cement staircase leading down the cliff is just a few cars away.

It's a great parking spot.

I turn the key and the engine shuts off and so does a commercial about dollar drink specials at a bar in Pacific Beach. Just a few days ago I wrote the event listing for their happy hour, but the memory of what I wrote is gone and I'm happy to have forgotten it.

Walking down the staircase to the rocks below I have a wide, panoramic view of the sea. It's dark green as dusk settles in, the waves backlit by the sun, clear like colored glass as they roll slowly to shore, curling over with the westward breeze which blows the whitewater back in a silent, spraying wash.

As I take the steps, holding onto the damp metal handrail to my right, I watch a surfer in a black wetsuit paddle into a wave and stand up as it begins to pitch forward. He squats a little and turns deeply at the trough of the wave then angles his board up the face of it and smacks the bottom of the board against the cresting lip of the wave, sending a dramatic fan of whitewash in the air like a peacock's tail.

At the foot of the staircase I walk across the rocky shore, jumping over the gaps of empty space between boulders, arms out for balance, before finding a good flat spot near the water to sit.

The waves hit the rock ledge below me and spray upward, but I'm just far enough away to watch it happen and keep dry.

At my feet, inches from the tips of my sneakers, is a tidepool. I stare into its small world—a lake the size of a puddle, with tiny gray crabs moving sideways, little green fish the size of jelly beans, jagged barnacles crusted to the walls next to clusters of black and silver mussels, anemones like alien flowers with their electric-blue tentacles, the carpet of bright green moss, the sea plants moving just slightly as if stirred by a breath—a beautiful world that is someone else's world, darkening now to a murk as the sun sets, a dim-lit quiet place where the things that happen in our world happen here too—procreation, the pursuit of food and the search for safety, a world of danger, survival, social life, fear, death, sometimes the water deep with the high tide, sometimes dropping low, exposing the tiny hills like the mountains of a relief map and valleys as small and narrow as cracks in a sidewalk.

Now the sun lowers into the sea and the world of the tidepool is dark. The sky over the sea is pumpkin orange with red and silver clouds that streak upward in thin, rippled strips like knife cuts gashed into the heavens—a Halloween sunset, an October sky.

"And now we shall go away from here," is the song I hear in my head as I stand up. "And now we shall go away from here/to find what is set out for us."

I turn, and with my back to the sea and the setting sun, I walk across the rocks to the staircase.

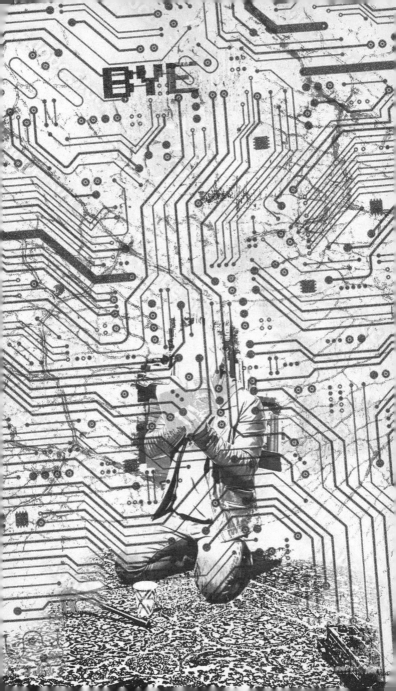

ABOUT THE AUTHOR

Born and raised in San Diego, California before leaving in his 20s to cross the continent many times by bus, car, and train, staying briefly in various American cities, Adam Gnade now lives on a six-acre homestead in the hilly cattle country outside the town of Tonganoxie, Kansas. His books and audio recordings of writing share characters and plotlines in an attempt to build a vast universe documenting how it was to live in the time that he was alive. The ongoing collected series is titled *We Live Nowhere and Know No One,* and continues in a variety of novels, novellas, and writing released on vinyl and cassette. Gnade runs the audio book-on-tape record label Hello America Stereo Cassette and tours regularly behind his releases, both domestic and abroad. *The Internet Newspaper* is his sixth novel.

ACKNOWLEDGEMENTS

Endless love to Elizabeth Thompson, Jessie Duke, Bran Black Moon, and Justin Pearson who helped directly in this book's creation, and to Bart Schaneman, Nicole Morning, and Nathaniel Kennon Perkins for advice on facts, media, technology, and language. Huge love to Yannis Philippakis of the band Foals and Dana Margolin of Porridge Radio for the blurbs they wrote for this one and for their new records, both of which have been a huge soundtrack this summer. Thanks goes out to Andrew Mears for being one of my truest, meanest friends. Thanks to Lora Mathis for the blurb and for the reminder to quit working sometimes which is a thing I'm very bad at. Serious Adam Gnade Hall of Fame awards go to the champions Jessie Lynn McMains, Erik Tinsley, Rich Baiocco, Andrw Fx, Becky DiGiglio, Erik Henriksen (and Henrik Eriksen), and Jon Nix for their blurbs, as well as for their beautiful work in general. Special and multi-tiered thanks to my heroes Liam and Jack Christian.

This song goes out to Gabe Serbian.

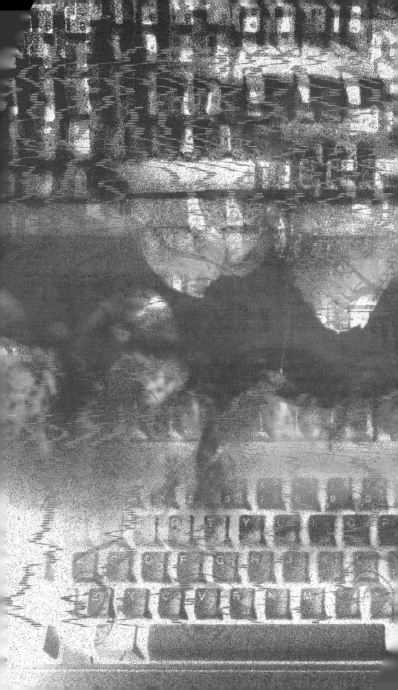

BOOKS BY

ADAM GNADE

AVAILABLE FROM THREE ONE G

AND BREAD & ROSES PRESS

After Tonight, Everything Will Be Different

Existing in the space between *Trainspotting* and *Like Water for Chocolate*, Adam Gnade's self-described "food novel" frames each chapter around a meal, and from there moves wild in all directions. *After Tonight, Everything Will Be Different* takes place in San Diego taco shops and rundown beach apartments, on the amusement park boardwalk at 3am and in cars bound for Tijuana and drunken glory. Like Proust's baroque autobiographical fantasies, this is a book rich with details and life. Gnade's youthful characters sink to hard drugs and deep depression as they navigate life at the end of the last century. They celebrate and they battle with their demons and throughout it all they eat. This is not a food snob's novel. Instead, Gnade writes about the pain and joy of life and the ways that common, everyday food is there with us at each step. This is a book of deli sub sandwiches, endless burritos, eggplant parmesan, the magnificence of good sourdough bread, of box brownies and Nacho Cheese Doritos, rolled tacos and the perfect tortilla. *After Tonight, Everything Will Be Different* is a raging, ecstatic, troubled book that shows a world of food and a world of life, each inextricable from the other.

"*After Tonight, Everything Will Be Different* is an excellent novel, an energetic tale of ambition, sorrow, and American hunger. Anthony Bourdain meets Roberto Bolaño." -Nathaniel Kennon Perkins, author of *Wallop*

2022, Fiction/Literature, ISBN: 978-1-939899-98-9

Float Me Away, Floodwaters

A pocketsize novel concerning modern farm living, wayward country punks, and the New Old West, Adam Gnade's *Float Me Away, Floodwaters* is a documentation of life on the margins of society, in the places forgotten by the city—the honkytonks and interstate campgrounds, the ghosts of cattle-towns and the desolate strip-malls. It's about ripping all the bullshit from your life and looking for things that make living worthwhile in the midst of poverty, political divisiveness, and a dying empire. "Float me away," the story says, away from loss and defeat, toward "somewhere without prisons up the road and white supremacists in the holler and long, daunting winters and that hard prairie wind that kicks up in the morning and doesn't quit all day." *Float Me Away, Floodwaters* is an ode to survival and place, home and away ...

"This book reads like a prayer that we can all somehow stay afloat in this country deluged with sadness and pain." —Bart Schaneman, author of *The Green and the Gold*

2021, Fiction/Literature, ISBN-13: 978-1-939899-37-8

This is the End of Something But It's Not the End of You

Adam Gnade's third novel is held up by a Springsteenian sense of hope and a desire for redemption, of finding glory and escape, friendship and love in hard times. Like Dickens' *David Copperfield*, Ferrante's Neapolitan tetralogy, and Karl Ove Knausgaard's *My Struggle* series, this is the story of a human life, kindergarten to adulthood, ratty beach apartment to bohemian party house, feverish basement to ramshackle farmhouse. Through the eyes of Gnade's protagonist, James Jackson Bozic, we see how life scars you, changes you as you fight to find a safe place for yourself. It is, in turn, a murder mystery, a love story, and a vast, sweeping, panoramic look at

America on the edge of collapse. It's a story of displacement, strange shores, new mornings. As James says in the book, "I thought of how sometimes in the midst of survival, life will jerk you away from your home, how it will push you out across the map, away from the people you love, or into the path of others." *This is the End...* is about scratching and clawing for a better, safer, more satisfying life, even as the sky comes crashing down.

"Reading *This is the End of Something But It's Not the End of You* is like having a drunken, late-night conversation with an old friend you haven't seen for years: freewheeling and wild, tender and warm, funny and a little bit sad, and altogether something you won't soon forget." —Juliet Escoria, author of *Juliet the Maniac*

2020, Fiction/Literature, ISBN-13: 9781939899354

Locust House

In his 2016 novella, *Locust House*, San Diego-born author Adam Gnade writes about his homeland in the tradition of regionalists Louise Erdrich and Willa Cather. Gnade's California is a place of border clash, of a glimpse of stormy sea from a top coastal hills or rollercoasters, of ratty beach apartments and punk shows. This is a story that asks, "What does it mean to hold fast to your dreams, ethics, and beliefs while the whole world tries to tame you?"

"*Locust House* is so dense, so angry, and so honest, and so everything that we need today to survive in the world." –Szilvia Molnar, author of *Soft Split* and *The Nursery* (forthcoming, Pantheon)

2016, Fiction/Literature, ISBN-13: 9781939899248

ALSO AVAILABLE

The Do-It-Yourself Guide to Fighting the Big Motherfuckin' Sad and *Simple Steps to a Life Less Shitty,* as well as the audio books backed by music: *Run Hide Retreat Surrender* (2005), *We are Ghosts and Bones Down Stone-Walled Wells* (2006), *Honey Slides* (with Youthmovies, 2007), *Palaces* (2007), *AMERICANS* (2013), *Greater Mythology Blues* (2013), *Life is the Meatgrinder that Sucks in All Things* (with Planet B, 2017), *Voicemails from the Great Satan* (with Demetrius Francisco Antuña, 2018), and *The World of Today and the World of Tomorrow* (2021).